SONG OF THE SEA

THE BLOOD BOUND SERIES

SABRINA VOERMAN

Song of the Sea: The Blood Bound Series, Book Three
By Sabrina Voerman
Published by Quill & Crow Publishing House

Edited by Tiffany Putenis and Lisa Morris

Cover Design by Fay Lane

Printed in the United States of America

ISBN: 978-1-958228-73-9

ISBN: 978-1-958228-72-2 (ebook)

Publisher's Website: quillandcrowpublishinghouse.com

For Kate Spofford,
I would not be the writer I am today without you.

THE BLOOD BOUND SERIES
BY SABRINA VOERMAN

Weaving the real world with fantasy, The Blood Bound Series features four books inspired by history and brimming with magic. Witches, werewolves, vampires, and sirens are at the helm of the series, featuring an overarching story that expands over centuries.

Packed with feminist themes and macabre storytelling, small connections between the first three books tie them together for the final book. The series features three books that stand alone and can be read in any order, each laying the groundwork for the finale.

Song of the Sea is the third book in The Blood Bound Series. Blood Coven is the first book, and the second is Ashen Heart, but all can be read as stand-alone novels.

A NOTE FROM THE PUBLISHER

Please consult the back of the book for content warnings. Index A is a helpful guide to understand the Blood Bound Series timeline. Index B includes a list of potential triggers.

NAME PRONUNCIATION

Æsa: iay-sa
Árelía: au-rel-ee-a
Eiríkur: ayr-ee-kur
Otávia: oh-taav-ya
Mihai: mee-hi

When Sól erupted
The country went hungry

The waters grew hot
And the Sirens did surface

The fabled Song of the Sea
Came out
For all to see

Man met Mermaid
Mermaid met Man
She came with gifts
Man came with greed

Prince Eiríkur placed them
Under protection
And won the heart
Of Árelía

So Prince of Land
Married Queen of Sea

Her beauty charmed him
But curiosity prevailed
So he ate away
At Árelía

Piece by piece
She went from wife
To delicacy

Myth to meal
Sacred to seasoned
Mermaids became a hunted species
Prince Eiríkur gained
A taste for the tail

Hiding deep
They became endangered

What was once
Song of the Sea

Was no longer

When the blood is spilled
The balance will return

— KÆ'VALE LEGEND

PROLOGUE

The Year of the Siren

The day the Sirens brought gifts for Man was one Árelía, Queen of the Sea, would never forget.

Months after the mountain Sól erupted and sent plumes of smoke into the sky, the detrimental damage still lingered. Humans scoured the beaches, searching for sustenance to feed their families. Sometimes, the dead ones washed ashore, and Man scrambled for them, fighting over their rotting corpses. The rest of the sea life hid too deep for Man to reach. For the Sirens, it was an easy task, though they did not eat the creatures of the Earth or Sea.

Sirens and sea life lived peacefully until then. Guilt billowed through Árelía as she held the wriggling creature that once trusted her never to harm it. Using a net lost by Man, she carried the fish to them. When Árelía saw the expression of those on the shore, her guilt dissipated. Most of them were women; they rose when they saw her and protectively grabbed for their young children who were helping them search. They were all skinny and frail. They were hungry. The women came forward, tentatively reaching out. Árelía could see the saliva dripping from their hungry mouths and knew she could not judge them for eating what they did; they were starving and would eat anything—even dead, rotting fish.

A young woman, no older than twenty winters, approached the Siren, wading into the water. Instead of grabbing hold of the fish in her hands, she touched her clammy cheek with soot-covered hands. It left a black mark along Árelía's skin, but she dared not move lest she startled her. The Queen of the Sea had thought they would be grateful for the food, and yet this woman was far more intrigued by the Siren than she was by the food being offered.

The woman spoke what sounded like a question.

Árelía did not understand her words, but they were beautiful.

A deep voice shouted across the shoreline, and moments later, a large pair of arms wrapped around the woman and ripped her away from the water. Jerking back away from the scene, she pushed deeper into the water but remained close enough to watch.

"Jakob!" The woman shouted and fought from the man's grasp. When he let her go, she splashed into the shallow water again. Her dress was soaked through, clinging to her bony frame, but she didn't care. Instead, she went straight to Árelía once again.

This time, Árelía reached out her hand. The woman took it in both of hers, holding it gently as though she were made of the very smoke Sól pushed into the air, as she would disappear should she grasp her too hard. They were so beautiful, legs and all: how could Sirens have been worried about Man when they were so gentle?

"For your family," Árelía spoke her language; though still soft like a lullaby, it felt strange upon her tongue above the water. The woman did not understand the words, though Árelía knew she would understand the gesture. Actions could transcend language. She handed her the fish, pushing it against her thin body.

She took it while the man, Jakob, watched with an air of caution. Leaning down, she pressed her lips to Árelía's cheek. Soft lips against damp flesh, it was a connection like she had never felt before. At that moment, with her advisors and Sisters awaiting in the waters below, she knew she made the right choice for both of their kinds. Man and Siren would work together.

The woman looked Árelía in the eyes, and she squeezed her hand ever so slightly.

She spoke again, then waited with curious eyes. She pointed to her chest and said, "Gyða."

"Árelía," the siren said.

"Árelía."

Árelía (The Year of Gluttony)

It was never forgotten: it was written into song and poem, told by storytellers around the country. They wrote about the food we brought them, how generous we were, never asking for anything in return. Our mistake—my mistake—was that I never demanded safety. They sought us out with boats and nets. Only once they had developed a taste for our flesh did I try to put a stop to the hunting. Instead of fighting back, I married a Man, Eiríkur. Their king. I did it to keep my Sisters, my lover, and my Daughters safe.

But none of us are safe.

Day by day, I am slowly becoming less as Eiríkur devours my flesh.

Otávia, my lady-in-waiting, enters my chambers. Her dark skin contrasts against the white garb she wears; silver and metal hoops hang from her ears and lips. One eye is dark brown, and the other is glassy blue; though she is blind in that eye, she sees everything.

"There are whispers of a Man—" she begins.

"I will not hear of any Man." I turn my head away from her; the promises of Man mean nothing to me.

She reaches her hand over my bathtub of a cage, then opens her palm. Inside is a medicinal mixture to ease my pain. It helps me sleep. It makes me forget that I am not even half a Siren anymore. My tail is nearly gone; like an hourglass, it will eventually run out. That's when Eiríkur will seek out others—if he hasn't already.

He will seek my Daughters and my Sisters.

This is why I allow him to take his time with me. This is why I have not accepted Otávia's offer of swift, painless death. How I crave it and desire it... Once Eiríkur is done with me, he will find the others. Another war will follow when my Sisters learn what has become of me.

"He is not quite Man." The Seer feeds me the medicine while I listen. "He is just a child, like her. But I have seen his future: I have seen the horrors he will face, the blood he will spill. In his future, there is nothing but pain. He will seek redemption for his failings in due time. He is the key, Árelía."

"What is his name?"

"Nikolai Sokolov."

1

ÆSA

The Year of the Black Tide

Æsa mourned for ten silent years.

Ten years passed since she had seen another Siren.

Ten years since she last saw the surface.

Her memories of Land were long since forgotten. Memories of the fires and the ships haunted her day after day. Massive ships once cut through the waves, nets dragged behind them and swept up sirens in their unforgiving, coarse bonds. Æsa's Sisters were caught and killed in droves as the Great War raged between Land and Sea. After Árelía was fully consumed by Eiríkur, the hunting began again. When the Sirens learned of the treachery committed against their Queen, they fought with everything they had. Until the Sea was drained of Sirens.

Æsa was desperately alone. All she had left were the memories of their bodies, Man and Siren floating in the choppy waters, sinking down into the ocean. When the last siren was hauled onto the deck of the ship named *Árelía* and the last Sister sank to the ocean floor with her spear in hand, the waters black with their blood, she knew it was over.

Before the final battle, they begged her to hide, and she begged to fight by their side. Her Sisters died protecting her while she survived.

But for what? Their stubbornness to fight for Árelía's dignity ended in a massacre on both sides, but Man prevailed for they were ruthless in their pursuit of Siren flesh. Life was not worth living when everyone you loved was dead. Æsa's survival instinct kept her alive for a decade of solitude. As the years went by, always hoping to see another Siren, that instinct, the need to survive, washed away.

Æsa longed for companionship, the love she once shared with her Sisters.

She longed for one breath of air above the water's surface. She longed to see Land once again, almost as much as she longed to see her Sisters, except Land still existed, and her Sisters were dead. Æsa could only remember the stories Sif and Eyvör told her of its beauty before Sól erupted, filling the sky with dark smoke, a dire omen of the darkness to come.

Glittering sunshine over the water—Æsa could not even picture it. Rolling hills of the land in the distance—such a green she could not imagine. Of all of it, she only remembered the fires. Fire on the water as the ships burned, the sounds of men screaming as flames seared their flesh, the salty ocean water doing nothing to ease their burns. Instead, the waters were a vortex of pain as the Sirens pulled them down, dousing their fiery skin only to fill their lungs with water. Æsa remembered their pain as though it was etched onto her own body.

For ten years, the temptation to rise to the surface battled within her. She imagined the netting wrapping around her, trapping her, cutting into her skin as it tightened. She imagined being pulled from the water and slammed down onto the hard wooden decks of the ships, Eiríkur's ships. Were they still up there scouring the Seas for the last of the Sirens to feast upon? Æsa looked down at her body, wondering if she would be good to eat or if they would keep her in a cage for display.

Cold ocean water caressed her, her pale flesh callous against the temperature. With each league closer to the surface, she felt warmth wrap itself around her. Though she could not see the sun as she moved closer to the world above, she could feel the drastic temperature change in the water. Something white and crescent-shaped stared down at her; she knew that she was near the surface. She stopped short. Ten years of hiding, ten years of safety. Why was she risking her life now? Her Sisters all died protecting her, fighting in the Great War, and finding a safe spot for her to hide and live out her life.

But was she really living?

Just one breath of air was all she wanted. She reached her webbed fingers to the slits in her neck. The flaps sucked in the oxygen from the water, gills that kept her alive beneath the surface. She was an arm's reach away from the surface, desperate to take a breath when she stopped. Æsa let out a sigh, bubbles billowing in front of her view, obscuring what little of the surface she could see. As the oxygen left her, she began to sink back down to the depths of the water. The Sea would always protect her, she reminded herself as she sank back down, accepting the life of loneliness once and for all.

Closing her eyes, she made only the end of her tail flicker, enough to remain floating in one spot. *Enough,* she told herself. She would swim back to the depths in a moment. *Do not let them have died in vain.*

Æsa did not hear the net as it came up behind her through the dark waters, for the boat was much further ahead, but she felt the coarse ropes touch her only when it was too late. It wrapped around her body, then was cinched tight as the hunters above pulled the expertly designed ropes. Digging into her flesh—flesh that had been untouched by anything but water and fire—the ropes burned as she desperately tried to swim down and away from the danger. Swimming only made it worse as it tangled around her, one arm getting stuck, her tail coiled up against her. The net was tiny now, no entrance and no exit. Like a giant hand, it wrapped all the way around her. Water rushed past her ears as she was forced up and out of the water. The change in pressure made her ears pop. Æsa gasped as the strangeness of cold air touched her body. Deep in her lungs, it felt icy, and she felt too full as she breathed it in.

The shouting of Man reached her ears as soon as the blood pulsing through her panicked body quieted down. It did nothing to lessen her fear. Hauled up in the air, Æsa hung above the water's rippling surface. Reaching her webbed hands out through the holes of the net did nothing but gain laughter from behind her. Clanging of bells—celebratory, most certainly—made Æsa cringe and try to cover her ears, but her arms were stuck in painful places. She opened her mouth to hiss as the net was brought right overtop of the ship. Instead of being dropped, she simply hung over the men as they all stared at her.

So many faces, more than Æsa had seen in ten years, stared up at her. Men slapped each other's backs, pointing and gesturing to her. They laughed abrasively at her panic, at each hiss of anger she spat out. Æsa knew her mistake: coming even that close to the surface would always be the death of her. Was this what she really wanted?

Soon she would be devoured by King Eiríkur, if he were still alive—how long had he reigned? Had he perished? She knew nothing of the world of Man except that which her Sisters told her, what they did to Árelía, and what little she had seen firsthand.

She would learn soon enough just how cruel they would be.

As she slumped painfully in her net, finally ceasing movement as nothing made her any more comfortable, she allowed herself to soak in the surface. In the distance, she could see the dark outline of the island. Kæ'vale, they called it. Within a few hours, she would be on Land, crated, and shipped away to be eaten. When her amber eyes found the sky, she noticed the crescent that she saw from underneath the water. It was not the sun; the sun was compared to fire—of which she was well acquainted. It was the moon gleaming down upon her with its icy smile. White as the dead shells at the bottom of the ocean.

White as the skeletons of her dead Sisters, whom she would soon join.

2

NIKOLAI

Soft clanging of metal on metal in the harbor paired harmoniously with the gentle sloshing of the waves over the bows of the boats and ships. Each boat—large and small—swayed side to side, rocking like a crib to put an infant to sleep. The gentlest of breezes could cause such, but there was a storm coming soon. October was edging closer to November, when the winds would pick up, and the weather would dance with danger. A stone's throw from the docks, where the wooden walkway turned into a muddy path, the sounds of grunts and shouting disrupted the calm and soothing sounds of the harbor.

Nikolai felt his opponent's fist connect with his jaw, a crack so loud that it rippled through his bones and into his brain. Foggy for a second, the burly man grinned wildly as the punch gave him the adrenaline he needed to finish the fight. When his opponent closed in to deliver the punch, he got himself in close range. Nikolai used this to his advantage, grabbing the back of the man's neck with thick hands and bringing his head down. At the same time, he brought his knee up so fast that when it came in contact with the man's face, he knew his nose was broken: he felt the crunch of cartilage. A hot gush of blood spilled down his leg, staining his trousers dark. In the darkened alleyway, the only light came from the onlookers' lanterns.

The fight was over, and the crowd shouted or booed as Nikolai shoved the unconscious man to the ground. The man slumped on his side, blood still pouring from his nose. Dogs pulled free from their owner's chains to lap up the blood, smelling the unconscious man's face to see if he still lived. The dogs let him be after that, as his heart was still beating—they would not feast on his flesh. Man's best friend could quickly turn against him.

Nikolai spat his blood onto the mud at his feet, feeling a loose tooth in the back of his mouth. The gums would heal, and the tooth would stay put; he'd lost a molar only once. Before the scent of the blood made his stomach knot, Nikolai stepped out of the circle of onlookers, who began passing coins to one another for bets won and lost. Nikolai would collect his pay and be on his way, but not before he listened in to what the dock workers had to say. This part of Kæ'vale was notorious for the Siren trade, which had dwindled to one or two found per year—supposedly. One had not been officially sighted in six years. Still, it was the best place to get one's hands on one, so long as Eiríkur's soldiers didn't find them first. Black Market Siren was in high demand, but low supply since the end of the war.

"My money." Nikolai reached his hand out, blood dripping from it. He felt sweat trickling from over his right eyebrow and reached up to wipe it away with the back of his tattooed hand, smearing blood over the lily tattooed there.

The man who ran the fights scowled at Nikolai. He withdrew a small leather pouch with coins from his vest and reluctantly handed it to Nikolai. The two had dealings together in the past. Nikolai never lost a fight, and he wouldn't hesitate to break a few fingers to get his full payment if that was what it took.

Nikolai grunted as he took the bag. Fingering the coins at a lightning-fast speed, he verified the payment. His blue eyes bore a hole into the man. "You're short."

"No." The man shook his head. "It's all there. You just don't know how to count. All you know how to do is fight."

"You are short," he repeated sternly, a thunderous look on his face.

The man forked over the few coins that he knew he was short, and the look on his face told Nikolai that he would never try that again.

"It's always a pleasure working with you, Nikolai." The man's voice was so sweet it made him shudder. The worst of people liked to cloak themselves in sweetness—he knew it too well.

As Nikolai turned away from the man, he beckoned to his dog, Kashmir. While Nikolai listened to the workers—the hush of voices, the rumors of what was new at the docs—Kashmir was trained to smell Siren. As men filtered into taverns to buy drinks with the money they had won in the fight, others slumped and grumbled curses over what they lost.

So far, there had been no whisper of any Sirens. The word on the street was that there were none left, that Eiríkur had taken them all for himself. Only those caged in circuses or secreted away in the homes of the rich remained. Whenever it caught Eiríkur's many ears on the street that a Siren was hidden in a home, his soldiers would raid until it was found. Not that anyone had seen the Mad King in many years.

Nikolai ducked into a tavern with Kashmir loping at his heels, hoping to drown himself in some ale. The tavern lanterns hung so low in the doorway that Nikolai had to duck to avoid banging his head against them. The ambiance was tense, only a few wary glances cast his way as patrons wondered if he might start another fight. Wiping the blood from his hands on his black trousers, he stalked up to the bar and flagged down the barmaid.

She wore her long brown hair pulled back in a braid, her stress-aged face fully on display. He made sure to tip her well, making sure to keep the money out of sight of the men who lost money to him. Not everyone could afford to be so generous with their coin, and those who could weren't. Nikolai, having come from nothing, understood that one extra coin in a pocket could mean living another day.

He lingered over his drink, listening to the patrons as they chatted, but the only thing anyone was talking about was the fight. Throwing back the dregs in his glass, Nikolai decided to wash up. He could no longer handle the scent of blood on himself. Leaving Kashmir where he slept under the table, he climbed the stairs to his rented room. He washed his face and hands with stale, cold water from the night before and changed into clean clothes. He slicked his messy blonde hair back. Feeling the sides of his head prickling against him, he knew he would need to shave again. Why he kept his haircut this way, a way he could be recognized, he wasn't sure.

Perhaps deep down, he was still the person he was running from.

Nikolai went back down to the bar for another pint, listening carefully. A short time later, he overheard the news he was hoping to hear. A few tables away, tucked behind a rowdy bunch who looked like they were re-enacting the fight from earlier, Nikolai noted two men leaning in close to one another. There was nothing on the table between them: no ale, nothing to eat. Instead of moving closer to hear over the ruckus of the other men, Nikolai focused, using his preternatural hearing to listen to the men, his hand scratching between Kashmir's ears.

"A live one?" The baritone-voiced man asked.

"Yes!" The other man sounded overly excited—he was speaking too loudly. His hair was white-blonde, and his features pale, glowing orange in the lantern light.

"Intact?"

"Mostly. A pretty blonde, too. Well, pretty as she can be with half a face."

"How long has it been?"

"Six years since the last one was found," the excited one said. "Or since, you-know-who got his hands on one. I saw a fin on the Market four months back, but who knows if it was a Siren."

"Keep your voice down," the deep-voiced man hissed. "Name your price."

Nikolai slid another coin underneath the pint glass he had been drinking from in the hopes that the barmaid would find it and store it away so she could escape one day, then left the bar before he could hear the cost. He knew he would never know what might happen to her—she could be murdered that night—but at least he had done what he could to better her life.

Outside again, Nikolai breathed in the icy air. He was impartial to the nipping chill of the wind, which had picked up since he entered the bar about an hour prior; it had been much colder in Osleka. Although Kæ'vale was not as cold as his homeland, winter still had a bite.

Down at the docks, he scoured the area for any sign of a ship capable of hauling a Siren. Years had passed since the last Siren sighting, but not many ships had gone out searching. Most had long since converted back to fishing and trades, and so those that had the capacity to hold a Siren and keep her quiet were easy to find. Nikolai and Kashmir were prepared, trained to search out Siren hunters. He needed to know what to prepare for if there really was a Siren for sale on one of these ships.

"I know you," a soggy voice called from the deck of a dingy.

It was the familiar accent that pulled Nikolai from his thoughts. Nikolai was tempted to keep walking, but his plan would only work if he went undetected. He turned on his heel; Kashmir stopped and sat as he was trained to do. Nikolai cocked his head to the side. "Unlikely; I am not from here."

"Neither am I," he said, this time in Oslekan. "You've been here before."

"Yes."

"You one of them Siren Hunters?"

"No." Nikolai remained still. "Street fighter."

"Ah, yes. Nikolai Sokolov, correct?" The stranger knowing his name confirmed his fears.

Nikolai tensed at his full name, and Kashmir looked up at him, waiting for orders. Many knew his given name—those who fought him and those who paid him. But otherwise, he was a nomad without a home and kin. He was no one. A chill caressed his spine as he wondered what else this strange man knew. Narrowing his eyes, he decided to abort his original plan and go back to his rented room at the tavern to overlook the water, watching for the Siren that would have to be moved from ship to carriage sooner or later.

"You've got me mixed up with someone else." Nikolai released a deep breath.

"They're coming for you, boy."

"Who?" Nikolai asked though he knew the answer.

The man grinned, flashing his teeth. Even in the dark, his sharp canine teeth were clear to Nikolai. He covered his teeth with his lips, watching Nikolai to gauge his reaction. Nikolai looked down at Kashmir, who was now on all fours, ears back and tail down, sharp teeth bared.

Nikolai rested his hand on the muscular head of his dog, nodding goodnight to the stranger and turning his back on the Vampire.

In his room above the tavern, Nikolai looked out the window, his tired eyes watching for any movement from the ships. He did not see the Vampire from the ship, but he could feel his presence. Heavy lids began to sink over his blue eyes as he watched everyone in and out on the docks, seeing nothing. He realized that he was hungry. Once he had something to eat, he could stay awake until sunrise.

3

ÆSA

After she had been hauled onto the ship, Æsa suffered. Only when she was entirely out of the water—for the first time in her life—did she feel the true weight of her own body. Her tail was dense with muscle, hardened by scales; its weight made hanging in the roughness of the ropes even worse. Double the rest of her weight, her tail and gravity forced her down. Her gills flapped uselessly in the air.

Æsa managed to slip into an uncomfortable sleep for a few moments at a time after her capture. These bouts of unconsciousness were minutes long at most, filled with memories disguised as nightmares. Each time she jerked awake, pain wracked her body. The ropes felt tight and coarse over her tender skin. They burned like the fire that scarred her when she was young.

As hours passed, the men came and taunted her, watching her writhe in pain. When they finally returned to do more than ogle and laugh at her, they reeked of something sour. Æsa did not know what it was, but her round nose crinkled as they lowered her toward the deck. When she was face-to-face with the men, she discovered it was their breath and sweat. Whatever they were drinking left a rancid scent in the air.

Man could be so ugly, so putrid.

Another scent floated toward her, far stronger than she had smelled before. One of the men held a bottle and a cloth. Two others, both with long hair and long beards, held spears to jab at her should she try to escape or fight them. Spears that once belonged to her Sisters. She hissed at them as they came near; how dare they attack her with her own Sisters' weapons.

One man cut the rope that held up the net, slamming Æsa into the wooden planks of the ship deck. She gasped as the feeling of colliding with something so solid rippled through her. All at once, the net opened, allowing Æsa to take the opportunity to escape. She was only a few meters from the edge of the ship. All she would have to do is slide herself along and over the edge; then she'd be free to swim as deep as possible, never to return to the cruelties of the surface and of Man.

Freedom was something she never truly knew—she could always taste it, but she could never touch it. But at least the lonely cage of the Sea would allow her to live.

A spear sliced her upper arm, severing her flesh and spilling her black blood. She hissed at the sharp intrusion, moaning in pain as she moved instinctively to cover the wound. In her moment of weakness, they struck. She responded with a slash of her hand, but by that point, the men were on her, pinning her down. A cloth came over her mouth; the sickly-sweet smell entranced her, and she felt her eyelids droop. Her tail lifted to buck them off, but unconsciousness consumed her.

Æsa woke up lying in a glass box full of sour seawater. It was not fresh, and it was a strange temperature—neither warm nor cold. She could only roll over to see that glass was on all sides of her. On the top of the cage, there were a few small holes big enough for her fingers to stick out to the second joint. Under the small amount of water, Æsa could hear everything. From heavy-booted footsteps to the voices speaking about her, all of it was noise that made her head pound. Each step rippled the water, the vibrations tearing through her.

"We need to decide." A man with black hair spoke loud enough that Æsa could hear. She listened intently; the words sounded strange, but she remembered from her Sisters teaching her the language of Man. "Eiríkur or Black Market... What's the word for either?"

"No one knows if Eiríkur is even alive; rumor is he died, but since he had no heir, his advisors don't want to lose their position by announcing his death. Black Market is in high demand, as usual. Those that are still out there are being sold to circuses. Only a few purists still seek them for food. I think we sell her to the circus, steal her back in a few months, and do it again."

"Can you get a hold of—er—Zimmer?"

"It's Zidler," the man corrected. He pushed back his white-blonde hair, almost as light as Æsa's. "Yes, we can have him here by midnight."

"We have to keep her quiet until then."

"She hasn't said a word," the blonde noted. "Maybe she has no tongue."

The black-haired man glanced over, then kicked the box. The thudding against the glass made all the water ripple like the waves of the Sea, slamming Æsa's head against the barrier behind her. She wanted to express her hatred, but she was too terrified to even scowl or hiss at them now. They had mostly ignored her once they got over the novelty of capturing her. Their attention was far more horrid.

"You have a tongue, Siren?" The man who kicked the box asked.

She blinked.

"You think she understands what we are saying?"

"Deaf and dumb," the man concluded, turning back to his companion. "It's a crying shame they got nothing but fins."

"They gross me out." The blonde shuddered. "Why Prince Eiríkur ever wed Árelía is beyond me, I tell you that much."

"I heard they have healing powers."

"They can suck the soul of any man who kisses them."

A laugh. "That explains why they call him The Mad King!"

Æsa listened to them talk about her, and part of her wanted to tell them that they were wrong. She could suck no souls if Man even had them, and she could heal no wounds. There was no power in her body, and she doubted her fins tasted as good as they claimed.

Feeling more and more cramped, Æsa began to breathe faster but felt as though no air was reaching her lungs; no oxygen was being extracted through her gills. She'd been in threatening situations before, but none of them compared to this. Not when all her Sisters had died, not when she was left alone for years, not when her tongue ceased to form shapes to make noise. She knew she had survived those hardships, but Æsa did not have the skills to get herself out of this.

Every other time her life was at risk, she survived because someone else died for her. Now, there was no one left.

Time seemed to stand still. Æsa began to understand that she needed to move to breathe through her gills, and since she was unable to do that, she was forced to bring her lips to the holes in the box and breathe the stale air of the ship. There was smoke—a Land smell that she did remember—but not the kind from the Great Wars. It stunk of something else entirely, and it made breathing hurt.

Would nothing be pain-free again?

Men came and went, but there was always one watching her.

Still groggy from whatever they had used to make her unconscious to begin with, Æsa stopped caring about time, Man, or Land and anything it held. Up a small flight of stairs that revealed it was still nighttime, the man who had kicked the box and taunted her about her tongue leaned in to talk to the man who was watching her.

"I've got a handful of respected buyers. Should I bring them here?" the blonde asked.

"How many have you told, you fool?"

"Sent word to Zidler, plus two others."

"And how do you know they are respected?" The man rose to his feet and ran his hands through his slicked-back, long black hair. It looked oily, like fish. "We agreed only on Zidler!"

"These are the risks of not having a buyer *before* we captured the Siren." The snarl in the blonde man's voice was enough to create a tense silence in the dark, smoky air. "Word spreads. Besides, competition will make them bid higher."

The man pinched the bridge of his nose, shaking his head. "Very well, when can they be here?"

"Within the hour."

4

NIKOLAI

Nikolai left his room over the tavern, silently descending the small stairway. Stopping abruptly, he narrowly avoided running into the barmaid where the stairs turned. She timidly ducked her head as if looking at him wrong would cause him to react violently. Yet she did not move out of the way. Nikolai suspected she had been in similar situations before, and he ached with sadness for her. "You do not need to look away. I mean you no harm."

"I know what you are," she mumbled.

Nikolai would have flinched if he wasn't used to such things. Some people were more intuitive to his kind, and the dirty looks he got were something he came to expect regularly. However, he had not expected the barmaid to look at him like that, her downcast eyes filled with what he thought was fear. He sighed, thrusting his hand into his coat and pulling out some coins. "For your silence, then. I will be gone by sunset tomorrow."

"I do not want your money." She spoke more clearly this time.

"I have more than I can spend," he lied. Money came and went; street fighting and the occasional hustle were no way to get rich.

"I wish to die," she said, finally looking into his eyes, her own filled with longing.

Had she looked at him in any other way, he would have tried to talk her out of it. He knew now that look was not fear of him and what he could do but desperation, a plea for what he could do *for* her. Many had asked Nikolai for death in the past, whether because they suffered physically or because they felt their lives were not worth continuing. It was rare for Nikolai to accept their request; he had enough blood on his hands. He saw in her what he often saw in himself. "Do you have a room?" he asked.

She nodded, turning back up the stairs, Nikolai following close behind. He gestured for Kashmir to sit at the base of the stairs, and the muscular dog did as he was told. Nikolai walked past his door and three others before the barmaid opened the door to her room. The closet-sized room was simple, with few personal mementos to show her personality. Nothing more than a bed with stained sheets, a scratchy blanket, and a wooden table and chair overlooking the docks through a small window. The plaster cracked, the paint peeling, and cobwebs hung in the corners.

"What is your name?" Nikolai asked, gesturing to the bed.

The young woman lay down and turned her head to look at Nikolai as he pulled the sturdy wooden chair up to the side of the bed. "Bría."

"I will make this as painless as possible," Nikolai promised. He whispered in Oslekan.

"What does that mean?"

"Your fight is over," he whispered, gently covering her eyes.

Her eyelids closed, and he felt her long lashes brush against his calloused palm. Her steady breathing surprised him, as most people would begin to panic at this point. At that moment, Nikolai realized that she truly wished for death, and so he brought his mouth to her neck without guilt, feeling blood pulsing through her carotid artery beneath his lips. Fangs penetrating her flesh, he fed while Bría's life slowly slipped away. She writhed once in pain until the pain itself disappeared. Mere minutes later, Nikolai threw his head back and gasped. The sloppy withdrawal made a small amount of blood spray on the pillow and dribble down his chin. His blonde hair was disheveled, and he slicked it back with shaking hands.

Out of his pocket, Nikolai withdrew a small phial, pouring most of the contents into her mouth. He placed the nearly empty phial on the bedside table beside her so that when someone found her in a few days when her corpse began to rot, they would believe she poisoned herself.

Nikolai only fed on those whose lives did not matter enough for anyone to investigate their deaths. So few cared when the poor died. They were merely fodder to those above them, Man or Vampire. No matter who he fed on, guilt left him empty.

Even if they did suspect, they would never find him. For ten years, he had been evading someone who very much wanted him found.

Donning his lengthy leather trench coat, he went to the streets once again. Nikolai felt more alive after feeding. He reached his arms out to the side when the rain began to fall, soaking in the chilled drops for a brief moment. He could still taste Bría's blood upon his tongue—honey sweet to a Vampire, a delicious aftertaste. He could feel the hum of energy from taking a life, and it thrilled him. When he came down from the high, he knew he had work to do. There was a Siren out there, and he needed to get to her before anyone else.

Two men with their heads leaned together just outside the tavern whispered of Sirens. Nikolai cocked his head to the side, hidden from their view, and listened. The ship *Árelía* was rumored to have a live Siren on board, and a bidding war was about to begin. One of the men headed down to the docks, leaving the other behind for a moment—staggered traffic would prevent suspicion if anyone watched the docks at this late hour.

As he suspected, the second man turned down in the direction of the docks—when he glanced over his shoulder to see if he was being followed, Nikolai ducked out of sight. Silently, he continued his pursuit. Grabbing the man from behind, he slammed his hand over the man's mouth and pulled him into an alley beside the tavern. Nikolai twisted his strong arms, snapping the man's neck like a twig. The gut-twisting crack had once made Nikolai sick to his stomach, but he was no longer bothered by killing—not men like this.

When your diet consisted of the blood of Man, you either overcame the feeling of taking a life or you took your own.

Nikolai pocketed the hefty sum of money the man had on him and left him against the wall of the tavern, hidden in the shadows. He headed toward the docks, seeking out the ship. Locating it with ease, he approached the first man who had been whispering to the one Nikolai just killed; he stood aboard the ship and glanced at Nikolai with concern but said nothing. Whether he was startled to see a new face or unsettled by Nikolai's very presence, he couldn't tell. Man was often torn between being entranced by Vampires and being terrified of them, all without knowing exactly why they felt that way.

As he waited by the ship *Árelía,* he was shortly joined by two other men—a man with hair so orange that Nikolai had to take a second glance and a slender, pompous-looking man dressed in furs. The man with hair like fire bore gaudy rings and used a cane despite not having a limp. Nikolai recognized him as Arthur Zidler, the ringleader of a circus that featured otherworldly creatures. None of them said a word to one another.

"Gentlemen, welcome," said the man aboard the ship when all three potential buyers arrived. His black hair was slicked back and braided. "I am Horik."

One by one, they boarded the ship, silent and ensuring they did not touch one another. Brawls and death were far too common in this kind of deal, and Nikolai was tense. He would win any fight against these older, out-of-shape men, but it might risk revealing what he was. He made sure not to show his teeth to Zidler. The infamous ringleader was known for buying and stealing all sorts of unique individuals. He didn't want the sword swallowers or acrobats. He wanted only the species that were bastardizations of Man—Vampires, Werewolves, Sirens, Witches, Seers, among others.

Nikolai scanned the other ships for the Vampire he had seen earlier, but neither the Vampire nor the ship he had been on remained in the harbor. Temporary relief filled him before he was guided down into the belly of the creaking ship. At last, his eyes were laid upon the Siren. Their eyes met, and he felt as though he had been punched in the gut.

5

ÆSA

Æsa was on her side, her webbed hands pressed to the edge of the fogged glass and her eyes searching for anything resembling humanity amongst the three men standing beside Horik. They nodded, speaking to each other about her but never addressing her. The fire-haired man stroked his pointed mustache, his soft green eyes curious and intrigued. The bald-headed, slender one licked his lips and made Æsa recoil, pushing hard against her tank.

Her sudden movement caused reactions from all but one man. He stood tall and broad, wearing a black leather jacket. He did not seem eager to be there. He did not look at her with hunger; it was as if he simply existed. His sandy yellow hair was slicked back but somehow still messy, the sides cut shorter than the top. While the other two looked pleased that there was a Siren available at last, this man looked upon her with disgust. His menacing blue eyes were reminiscent of how Eiríkur's eyes were long ago described to her.

She was most terrified of him.

"Shall we begin?" Horik suggested with a gesture of his hand, flaunting Æsa like she was a prize to be won.

"What happened to her face?" The orange-haired man asked, his thick accent different from any Æsa had heard before.

"This may very well be the last siren," Horik reminded them. "Does it matter what happened to her face?"

"It does matter," the man argued. He thrust his hand out, gesturing towards Æsa like she was something foul. "I cannot display her if she is burned."

"Then you may take your business elsewhere, Zidler," Horik snapped.

The man, Zidler, hushed after that, but a scowl remained on his face.

The bald one spoke up. "Why not ask her?"

"She does not speak, Magnus," Horik admitted.

"Charred and speechless?" Zidler threw his hands up in the air. "A siren that cannot sing! What good is she?"

"If you do not wish to buy, you should leave," the frightening man growled. His accent, too, was unfamiliar to Æsa.

"Forgive me, Horik," Zidler spoke to Horik, not the one who addressed him. His voice was now sharp and determined, determined to outbid the others. "I simply like my product to be perfect."

The one with ice-blue eyes shook his head briefly. Relief filled her when he looked away.

All these men talking about her and how valuable she was while mentioning that she was not good enough for them... It made Æsa want to wither away. She knew she had been burned during the Great Wars, but she never saw herself. Instinctively, she reached up and touched the part of her flesh that had always felt different.

"And what use do you have for her?" Magnus asked the blue-eyed man. "Zidler for show, me for feasting, and what about you? Who are you anyway?"

Horik turned his attention to the blonde and said, "I spoke with another man earlier, and I do not see him here now. Are you an informant of Eiríkur's, perhaps?"

"My name is of no importance, and what I want with her is none of your business. In the trade of Black Market Siren, some men do not make it as far as the bidding. Sometimes," he paused, scowling, "the competition frightens them off."

His answer seemed to satisfy Horik. "Let's get on with it then, shall we?"

When the bidding began, Æsa's glance flitted between all the men. They spoke quickly, and their accents made Æsa struggle to understand what they were saying—not that she understood money and how it worked. Was she going to be worth a lot, even with all her burns? She doubted it, but it didn't matter how much she was sold for, at least not to her.

Eyeing her options as they threw meaningless sums, she wondered who the worst would be. The bald one already claimed that he would be eating her, so she didn't want him to win her. There was the orange-haired man, Zidler, who spoke playfully but scowled at her burns—he'd put her on display for everyone to ogle her. But she would be alive, and Æsa considered that the best option.

The remaining one scared her most of all. Clad in all black with broken flesh upon his knuckles, he did not look like someone who would do her anything but harm. But then, she trusted no Man would not harm her.

In his piercing eyes, Æsa saw something horrid; he looked like the type who might torture her, poison her, and try to give her legs like they said Eiríkur did to Árelía. She didn't want to end up in his clutches. Of course, she had no say in what was going to happen to her all because she wanted to see the surface. Temptation and curiosity got her caught, and it was only a matter of time before she was killed.

The bidding came to an end, and Æsa tuned back into her surroundings. Her gaze quickly landed on the blonde—he looked as though someone spat in his food. The scowl on his comely face could make anyone shudder in fear, but it brought Æsa relief. Of all the men in front of her, he was the one she did not want to be sold to.

The bald one grumbled, and she felt another wave of relief as she realized she would not be eaten, just put on display. As she watched Zidler open a bag of rattling coins, she felt the blonde's piercing blue eyes on her. Forcing herself to look, she brought her gaze back to him, but he was gone.

Magnus walked over to Zidler and slapped him on the back while shaking his head. "If you ever grow bored of her, if she does not bring in the viewers you hope, you know how to find me, yes?"

"But of course." Zidler was smiling like a child given a gift. "If you come to the show, I'll give you discounted entry."

"How gracious."

6

NIKOLAI

She was burned into his memory now.

Nikolai knew that even though he lost the bidding war for her, he would not give up his goal of obtaining the Siren. When he had boarded the ship, he had already known he would not win against Zidler. The Ringleader was too powerful and rich to be outbid, but Nikolai had not joined the bidding war to win. He joined to confirm if the Siren was real: it was not uncommon for con artists to fake them. This one was real; there was no denying that. From the few missing scales of her tail, the burns on her face, to the bones through the bridge of her nose—a Siren trademark—there was nothing false about her.

Nikolai had been able to smell her blood as soon as he stepped into the ship's belly; her arm had been cut not long before Nikolai had arrived, maybe a few hours at most. That was one of the most obvious signs she was real, though only a Vampire could sense it. The bitter scent of a Siren's blood was so strong that Nikolai almost had to walk out of the ship then and there. But he had held strong and avoided breathing through his nose. The scent of Siren blood was nothing new to him; he had learned everything he could about Sirens upon his arrival in Kæ'vale a decade ago. After the death of his mother, he was desperate to find purpose again.

He strode along the docks, his long strides covering more ground to get out of sight quickly. The sun would be rising soon, and he had to seek shelter. But he stopped when a familiar face appeared.

Upon his small boat once again, the Vampire he had spoken with earlier said, "You better run, boy."

"I've been running my whole life," Nikolai told him. It was just like his brother to send someone to taunt him, to remind him that he would never stop hunting him.

"Sooner or later, they'll find you."

"I look forward to the day they do," Nikolai said, lying through his teeth. He knew who was after him, and he knew it was not a fight he would win. The day they found him would be the day he died. While he was not entirely scared of death, now was not the time. He craved the release of death, but just not yet—he had more to accomplish first.

"I am but the messenger, Nikolai." He held up his hands, implying his innocence.

"What is your name?" Nikolai inquired, turning so he was fully facing the other man. He latched his fingers together in front of him, glancing at the horizon. The sun would rise soon, and Nikolai and the strange gentleman would have to disappear. When it set again, he would begin his hunt for Zidler and his traveling freak show.

"Vlad," he replied. "You better run, Nikolai—the sun isn't the only thing coming."

HE RETURNED to the inn and packed up his few items, leaving with Kashmir. With Bría's body only three rooms down from him and with Vlad lurking in the docks below, Nikolai needed to find another place to rest. He was lucky: this time of year, accommodations were easy to find. Regardless, he knew he would not rest well.

When the sun set the next day, Nikolai was on the move. Kashmir close at his heels, Nikolai took only a small bag and set off.

As midnight approached, Nikolai slipped into a tavern, hoping to catch word of Zidler's circus. Other than the knowledge that Zidler was going west—something he overheard from a passerby—he had no idea how long it would take to catch up. Likely not long, as Zidler had a circus to pack along with him, while Nikolai only had himself and his dog.

Only one thing was in his favor: Zidler would keep the Siren alive for the show, though in what kind of shape, he didn't know. He wanted to get his hands on her before Zidler went public with the fact he had a Siren. It was dangerous for him to do, as word could easily get to the castle. Waking Eiríkur from his six-year silence would stir up trouble for everyone.

Taking a seat by the bar, Nikolai kept his head down, his dog at his heels. Most people wouldn't tell Kashmir to leave; they didn't even notice him most of the time. When the dog curled up at Nikolai's feet, he was silent and took up little space. The male bartender approached Nikolai with a casual saunter.

"Good evening, what can I get you?" the bartender asked.

"Nothing to drink." He waved his hand; he needed a clear head, and he was already groggy from lack of sleep. "Information, if you have it."

The man glanced around, then nodded. The bar was empty enough that he was able to spare a moment to chat. "Go on."

"Zidler's show."

"Zidler's Wonders." He stroked his bushy gray beard. "He is taking his show to K'via."

With lips pressed tight, Nikolai pondered this. K'via was the capital of Kæ'vale—perfect for a circus show, for selling and trading, for invention, for meeting new faces, and for hiding from old ones. However, it was also where Eiríkur resided if he was still alive. Hiding a Siren right underneath his nose was either a death wish or a brilliant idea. Knowing Zidler, it was probably going to be brilliant. The rest of the world had moved on from the Great Wars and the hunting of the Sirens, believing them to be extinct. They carried on with their lives as though it had never happened. To hear that a circus with a Siren was coming to town would draw in the skeptical, but most wouldn't pay to see what they believed to be a con.

Nikolai wondered how long Zidler was planning on staying in Kæ'vale before he went back to the mainland. Not long, he presumed. One, maybe two shows in the Siren capital of the world, then off to inland places where most didn't even know they existed. Of course, there were other Sirens in the world, but they were scarce. Nikolai learned of the *Rusalka* when he was a child from books his mother read to him. They told stories of Siren-like creatures who haunted the lakes they drowned in; some of the fables even claimed a kiss from one could cure all ailments. He had never believed this, but he knew someone who did.

"Do you have any carriages and horses for sale?" Nikolai inquired.

"I do..." He nodded towards the back door.

With Nikolai following him, the bartender opened the door to the stableyard behind the tavern. A few broken-looking carriages sat there in desperate need of the blacksmith's attention. There were a few that might make most of the trip to K'via without breaking down. Nikolai could manage to fix up a few things along the way; that was no issue. Time was his main concern. It would take two weeks at best to reach K'via—faster without the carriage, but he needed it for protection against the sunlight. The bulk of his travels would not offer the safety of inns and other shelters.

The bartender watched him closely as he eyed the best-looking carriage. All black, wide enough to hold a tank for the Siren, with only one small window at the front. There was no seat within; this carriage had been used to carry the dead. It would be crowded with himself, a Siren, and Kashmir in there during daylight hours, but it would do for now.

"It'll cost you," the man told him as Nikolai's determined expression made it clear which carriage he was interested in purchasing.

Nikolai grinned, then cracked his knuckles. "Give me an hour."

7

ÆSA

Æsa did not know how much time had passed. All she knew was the hunger in her belly and the infection developing in her gills, where it itched and throbbed, making it hard to swallow. Her skin was sallow, and her eyes struggled to remain open, the sour waters stinging them.

In the Sea, she never knew if it was day or night. Hiding so far underneath in the safety of the deep, her eyes adapted to perpetual darkness. She guessed her age by the changes she felt and by the seeping loneliness she endured, never able to truly mark the passage of time.

She knew time had gone by—she could feel that much. Her body grew weaker since she couldn't move within her cage, which had grown filthy. Algae was blooming in the corners of her glass cage and dead fish floated on the surface of the water where she needed to put her mouth to breathe. She did not eat fish, yet they continued to give them to her. They knew nothing of what she was or what she needed to survive. Æsa was certain that she was going to die in her glass cage well before she was put on display.

When Æsa was close to starving to death or would otherwise perish from inhabitable conditions, she was finally released from the tank.

Into another.

Dumped from the algae-infested one, Æsa found herself in a vertical box. Larger than her previous tank, she was able to move around and breathe through her gills instead of pushing her mouth against a small air hole. The water did not reach the top, allowing her to rise above it should she wish to. There was enough room for her head and shoulders to rise below the locked lid. After she took in her new surroundings, soaking in the fact she could move, she realized there were people watching her. Her eyes scanned the room, landing on Zidler with his arms crossed over his chest. Eye to eye, as he walked up to the edge of the cage, he inspected his new showpiece.

Waving someone over, he turned his attention to the large man beside him. "I want eyes on her at all times, Brutus. Day and night. No one comes in or out without my permission. I have no doubt someone will try and take her from us while we're here. 'The Last Siren on Earth'—that is how we will advertise her."

"Yes, sir." Brutus nodded. He was very muscular, his arms so large that he couldn't rest them against his body. His head was shaved bald, smooth, and shiny under the glow of the lighting.

"I want to start the show as soon as possible." Zidler began to walk around the cage. "She's too skinny. We'll need to fatten her up, but she has not eaten anything we've given her. We can't have the star of our show starving to death, can we?"

"No, sir," Brutus replied curtly.

Zidler then addressed Æsa. "You must speak. You must have a name. Tell us, Siren."

Æsa stared, her tongue feeling heavy like rocks inside of her mouth. No matter where she put it, it felt uncomfortable. Too fat, too slimy, too firm. The language of her Sisters was meant to be heard under the water, but when Árelía married Eiríkur, they learned the language of the Land, too. Æsa glanced at the open space of air in her cage but chose to remain where she was.

Vertical in her box, Æsa moved only the base of her tail and her hands to keep herself upright. Each movement swished the water and made loud rushing noises. The Sea was so vast that she never was bothered by these sounds—she never heard them over the beautiful crash of the waves and the rush of the undercurrent. She longed for the Sea in the way she once longed to see Land. Filled with regret, she was sure she would die this way.

"Why will you not speak?" Zidler was already growing impatient, his face turning a dark shade of red, as though his orange hair was leaking down into his wan face. He slammed his gloved fists against the glass.

Æsa opened her mouth and cried out, a flurry of air bubbles covering her vision. Her webbed hands darted to her sensitive ears, and she cringed until the rattling stopped. The vibrations settled down, but she could still feel them throughout her body. She was shaking, terrified of what was to come. Such a minor disruption had upset her so viciously; surely Zidler would come up with other horrible methods to make her do what she was told. She would allow herself to be put on for show; she would wade in the water for the revenue it would bring Zidler, but she would not smile, and she would not speak.

"At least tell us what you'll eat, dear." Using a tone that was sickeningly sweet, Zidler felt less and less human. His gloved hands were pressed against the glass, spread open, and he stared at her through them. "You do not eat the fish we give you. Vegetation?"

Æsa nodded, acquiescing to prevent herself from starving. Self-preservation will always be a part of her, as she was born in turmoil and raised in war. She understood how to survive each day on her own. So long as she ate and was able to move around, she would get through this. She wondered if surviving in this cage to be put on display was worth living for. Was it any different from the despair and loneliness she felt in the Sea?

At least then I was free, she thought sourly.

After she had confirmed her food source, she was left alone—except for Brutus. She embraced the silence and the darkness. Sleeping proved difficult in her new space, so she sank to the bottom and rested her head against the cold glass. After eating, her stomach bloated—she had been starving for days. Nevertheless, she rested well regardless of discomfort.

She woke with a kink in her neck, but that was the least of her worries. Only one light was on, a lantern flickering ominously a few feet from her cage. Zidler sat in a chair beside the lantern, holding a long piece of wood with multiple threads of leather attached to it. Æsa had never seen anything like it, but she could tell it was not something she wanted to become familiar with.

"You are a true beauty." He spoke softly, different from before. It was far more terrifying. "Despite your disfigurement, you will bring in viewers from around the world. I do not wish to disfigure you further, but should you disobey me, I will not hesitate."

Æsa stared into his cold eyes and nodded her head once.

"Very good," he praised. "First question: do you speak?"

Æsa shook her head. Moving to the edge of her cage, she pressed either palm on the glass and looked at Zidler as he had looked at her. There needed to be an understanding between them if she was going to live. She was determined to survive, even if she were to live out her days as a display piece for all the world to ogle. What she wasn't going to do was speak—it would give Zidler, or anyone else, far too much power over her. They'd torture her until she gave up the other Sirens, even if Æsa didn't believe there were any left aside from her.

One Siren left in the world, and she was burned and mute.

"Second question: can you speak?"

Æsa shook her head again.

"I do believe I paid too much for you." Zidler laughed. It appeared he believed her. "Third question: will you do everything you are told? Will you obey?"

Æsa nodded reluctantly.

8

NIKOLAI

For five nights, he rode, passing black sand beaches and navigating the tricky road. For five days, he slept with only the blacked-out carriage to protect him. By the third night, Nikolai was sure he was being tracked. Whoever was following him was loud enough to draw his attention. He kept a steady pace to remain ahead of his pursuer; the distance he made each night was just enough to remain safe for the time being. Despite all the enemies he made throughout his lifetime, he knew who was sending people after him. His run-in with Vlad nearly confirmed it, and he knew it wasn't long before the real threat grew bored. It wouldn't be long before he was face to face with his past.

Nikolai grew restless on the sixth night. It had been a while since he'd fed. Generally, a Vampire ate nightly, but while traveling, it was difficult to find someone during the night so he could eat without being scorched to death by the sun. At some point, there would be someone he could find. It was those nights when he was hungry and desperate that he did not care who he attacked. Instead of acting recklessly, as he might have in his youth, he allowed his pursuer to reach him at last.

When the sun set, he left the carriage where it was and waited.

Nikolai pulled a slab of bloody meat from the back of the carriage.

Slicing the meat into cubes that were a comfortable size for Kashmir, he began to whistle a tune he recalled from his childhood. Though he preferred to forget his early years, the tune always clung in his mind, a melancholy song his mother used to sing. Kashmir sat patiently at his feet with one ear perked up. Tail wagging, the dog began to drool at the sight of the meat.

"Come on up, Kash." Nikolai patted the carriage, and the dog leaped up. Placing the meat into a bowl, he gave it to Kashmir, who ate it in one hungry gulp. Though Nikolai went from feeding to feeding while going hungry in between, he made sure his dog was never hungry. As Kashmir ate, he waited, listening. At first, only a raven in the distance made any sound. Then, footsteps.

"Guess I should have known you would be waiting for me." A dark figure walked down the rugged path. "They told me you were intuitive."

Like a bad smell, his voice made Nikolai cringe. Above them, dark, threatening clouds obscured the moon, which had prevented Nikolai from seeing the man before he decided to announce his arrival.

"I have to admit, I do not even know who I'm waiting for," Nikolai said, his voice steady.

Nikolai leaned forward, the knife still in his hand. His sleeves were rolled up to his elbows, revealing only the lily tattoo. His other markings were easy to identify, so he kept his upper arms and back covered most of the time. He recalled getting them so many years ago and how, at the time, it almost felt like he was bonding with his brothers. Now, it was a brand permanently stamped on his flesh.

"Why does this not surprise me, Nikolai?" the man asked mockingly.

Nikolai squinted to see the man. Hunger rumbled within him, and he knew it might affect the outcome if it came to a fight. The lantern beside Nikolai flickered. Glancing cautiously at Kashmir, he clicked his tongue twice. The dog hopped out of the carriage and loped around to where the horses were tied. Out of reach of the stranger, Kashmir would be safe if Nikolai needed to start—and finish—a fight tonight.

"So, who is it this time?" he asked the stranger. The man before him—now only a few meters away—was sun-kissed with wrinkled skin.

"The Brotherhood is missing a brother," the man said smoothly. "They sent me to bring you back."

His deepest fear was confirmed: after ten years, Roman was finally closing in. Now that it was true, Nikolai needed that Siren more than ever before.

Scowling at the thought of his brother, Nikolai stood from the end of the carriage and unsheathed his knife before the stranger could see it. Closer now, he suspected this man was just that—a Man. Not a Vampire, not part of the Brotherhood. A pawn in the giant game of chess that Roman played at all times. A man desperate to become something else. No doubt Roman had promised to change him into a Nightwalker and told him lies about Vampires so that the man would do anything to become one. To join the Brotherhood, a crumbling empire.

But there was nothing glamorous about the life of a Vampire. Death by sunlight meant living only at night, and living only at night meant being alone for eternity. That, plus having to drink blood for a food source, made friendships and relationships impossible. A Nightwalker's only friend was another Vampire, and Nikolai had found them a rough bunch that he didn't care to associate with anymore.

"What did my brother promise you?" Nikolai asked, stepping closer again. The lantern was behind him and gave off very little light, but he knew where the man was. That was all he needed.

"Eternity, power, women."

"Women, yes. Even willing ones. Power...perhaps." Nikolai knew his brother. Roman fed this very lie to another once before, and she believed him. Vampires could charm nearly anyone into their reach before they drained them of their lifeblood. "You believe Vampires live for eternity?"

"How can they not?" His voice raised with excitement. "Feasting upon the living will give one life."

Nikolai scoffed. "Do men who eat animals live forever? We are no different from Man, except that we drink blood and have a *slight* dislike of the sun."

"Roman told me you would try to convince me otherwise. That you were a liar. He has proven himself to me—the Witch who resides with him has not aged a day in a decade!"

"I am no liar." Nikolai kept his calm, his thoughts trailing to the Witch. Nikolai met her once before and was disappointed she didn't heed his warning about Roman.

They were an arm's length apart now. Nikolai continued, "Roman will tell you everything you want to hear to make you do his bidding, trust me. You do not want this life."

"How could I not?"

When he realized there was no reasoning with this man, he lunged forward to grab him. The stranger withdrew his own knife. Seedy and jumpy, he was able to dodge Nikolai and ducked under his grasp, spinning behind him and stabbing Nikolai in the shoulder with the small dagger. Nikolai roared in pain, jerking away from it. Pulling out his own knife, he breathed out coolly, and they began to circle like two wolves, ready to fight for the last of the meat.

Nikolai sidestepped and swung out his leg. He tripped the man and stepped over him. The man raised his knife to slice at Nikolai, but he grabbed his wrist, snapping it backward. The crack of bone shuddered through the quiet night, and Kashmir whined in the distance. The man screamed, his radius snapped, jutting through his flesh. Nikolai's sharp canine teeth penetrated the soft, worn flesh of the man's throat, and he felt the rich iron flavor hit his taste buds.

The sweetest blood was from the throat—the jugular—and Nikolai savored every second of it as the man writhed in pain but could do nothing to stop his inevitable death. He almost moaned in satisfaction as he tasted his first fresh blood in days, scarcely managing to control himself as he finished his meal.

Kneeling in the dirt, Nikolai wiped his mouth and shoved the corpse aside. He hadn't even learned his name, and he did not care. He was just a pawn in Roman's game. Rising to sturdier legs than before, he took a deep breath, absorbing the cold night air into his lungs. A whistle escaped his lips, the very tune he had been whistling earlier.

9

ÆSA

"It is time for the world to see you," Zidler said. He stood beside Æsa's cage, leaning against it, pulling his mustache in a repetitive motion. He was not looking at her but at the great tent that surrounded her. He looked longingly toward the flaps, which were latched shut.

"Together, you and I can remind the world of the beauty they tried to destroy. Killing you, hauling you up from the depths, *eating* you. Disgusting. How they dare desecrate such beauty. These...these monsters have no concept of art!" Zidler's voice was raised now, his body trembling with rage at those who would rather eat Æsa than display her.

Æsa listened, but she could not sympathize. All she could do was tread the murky water around her and wonder how Zidler was any different from the others. Her mind drifted back to the bald man who wanted to eat her. Would he have killed her first and then eaten her fast? Or slowly, like Eiríkur, who took his time to devour Árelía.

Zidler suddenly pushed himself off the cage and clapped his gloved hands together. "Let the show begin!"

He paused to turn towards her, glancing at her once up and down. "Do not disappoint me."

Zidler left, unlatching the tent flaps and slipping out without allowing anyone a free glance. Brutus entered while the other man, Ansel, stood at the entrance to prevent anyone who didn't pay from getting in. Glancing around at the striped circus tent, yellow like the sun and orange like Zidler's hair, Æsa waited to be displayed. To be seen by more people than she had seen in her life.

Eventually, the tent filled up with thirty or so people staring at her, gasping, covering their mouths, and whispering to the person next to them.

Æsa heard their words, but they meant nothing to her. Since the day she was taken from her beloved Sea, she thought of nothing but being released back into it. To feel the waves crash over her, the wide spaces where she would be free to swim and swim. If she ever made it back there, she would swim so deep the light would never touch her skin again, and Man would never see it again.

They did not deserve to see her.

Loud music played through the air, making the water vibrate in a vicious thrum, pounding against Æsa's ears. It was joyous music, but it sounded like pain to her. Music of the Sea was that of voices, collective and beautiful—a lullaby that would drown all else out. This was crude and sharp, too loud, too fast. She longed for it to stop. She longed to be hidden away from these prying eyes.

Occasionally, the tent flap would open, and Æsa would see the open field, catching glimpses of fire spinning around before being devoured by someone. She was curious about all the creatures and unique individuals in the circus, but she did not wish to be a part of it. But as she watched the Fire-Eater, she wondered how he dared get that close to the flames. Her hand grazed her burnt face.

Someone tapped the glass, their meaty fingers making Æsa recoil. Baring her teeth, she hissed. Many of the spectators stepped closer, eager to see her make any motion aside from the occasional flick of her tail or webbed fingers so that she could remain upright. Women looked at her bare breasts, too intrigued by the strange creature to look away. Men ogled her. For hours, they stared at her, tapping the glass to get a reaction from her, and when she stopped giving them anything aside from a forlorn look through her glassy eyes, they began to filter out of the tent.

Alone at last, Æsa sank to the bottom of her tank and wished she could see anything other than the yellow and orange tent around her. But the next face she saw showed no joy, only anger. Zidler stood in front of her cage, looking at her while his head shook side to side.

"We talked about this, did we not?" he asked. "I asked you only to smile, to look beautiful. To look like my prize, not my prisoner. I asked that you not disappoint me, and yet you did."

Zidler continued, "I have a complete collection now, but you are not worth the effort if you do not do your part. I have a docile Vampiress who dances for my viewers. I have a Half-Werewolf trapped in a faulty transformation—half man, half dog. His life is very difficult; he fits in nowhere in this world. But I gave him a home, a place to stay. So long as he does as I say. And Siren, he does as I say. I have given you a *home*."

Æsa felt fear run through her veins like ice, but she refused to show it. To keep her terror concealed, she clutched her hands tight so that her sharp-pointed nails dug into her palms. She looked away from him because she knew what was coming next. With a flick of the hand, Zidler got his two guards, Brutus and Ansel, to move her glass cage. It was wheeled outside the tent, and Æsa spotted that bright white moon in the sky. She gazed upon its ethereal beauty with thoughtful eyes, absorbing its pull. The moon had the power to change the oceanic tides; perhaps it could change her course.

Suddenly all the water was being drained and the front of the box opened. Æsa could not stop herself from sliding out of the cage along with all the water, and she slammed into the muddy grass below. She clawed at the ground, trying to move, but her tail felt too heavy. Making it only one body length along the ground, she felt something heavy on her fin and cried out in pain. Brutus stood on her fin, keeping her in place with a wicked grin. She could tell by the glint in his eyes that he enjoyed this.

Ansel handed Zidler the whip.

Æsa made herself a promise that she would never speak and would never smile. No matter what they did to her, she would not give them that satisfaction. Laying prone with her arms holding her up, she stared at Zidler. When a grin spread over his lips, intrigued by her spark, she watched him take one step closer before walking around her. This time, she did not turn to watch; she knew what was coming next. A warning crack of the whip made her flinch, her muscles tensing for a moment, betraying her fear.

Zidler chuckled, and then the whip came crashing down on her back. The tension in her muscles made it hurt even more. Like a thousand jellyfish stings, the strike sent pain through Æsa's entire body. Her arms collapsed, and she crashed into the mud. Hands covering her face, she gasped in pain. The whip retracted and came down a second time. Her entire back throbbed in agony, multiplying as she was hit again and again until the skin broke open, her dark black blood oozing out.

Only then did Zidler stop and walk around to face her. "Brutus, lift her. I want to look into those pretty eyes."

A large hand wrapped around her neck from behind. Brutus stood over her tail and lifted her up. Struggling to breathe, Æsa clawed at Brutus's arm around her throat, trying to pry him away from her. She was unable to break free, air hardly making it into her lungs. Tears slid down her cheeks. Zidler crouched in front of her, still the whip in his hand.

"There are rumors stating Sirens can only live a few hours outside of water." He made a clicking noise with his tongue. "I have been told it is like dying of thirst. Shall we test that?"

She simply raised her lip, revealing her sharp teeth.

"Tie her up, Brutus."

10

NIKOLAI

K'via was busy even at nightfall, and Nikolai worried that he would be recognized, though it had been six years since he had been there. Wearing his black jacket to cover his tattoos and wraps over his bloodied hands, he slipped into the first tavern he found. The journey had been exhausting, but it would only get more difficult once he had the Siren.

There were signs all over the place for Zidler's circus. Nailed to the wall, lying in the mud just outside the tavern, they whipped in the light wind as if beckoning Nikolai to go view the marvelous Siren. Her image was burned into his memory, but he didn't long to see her. None of the posters said where the show was being held, keeping clientele low enough in numbers that only the most curious would expend the energy to seek it out.

"What can I get you?" A Black woman approached him, metal and tattoos covering her body. She had a thick accent that seemed to give her voice power. Around her wrists were tattoos, snakes curling up her forearms, with an open eye on top of her hand. Different pieces of metal dangled from her ears, clinking together like a tiny symphony.

"Ale, please." Nikolai held on to common courtesy and politeness—

he didn't want to drink, but sometimes, it was the only way to get information.

"You're not looking for a drink, are you?" she asked as she grabbed a glass to fill. No matter where she stood, it was as if her strange eyes were always on him. One was dark brown, the other was milky blue—even the blind one seemed to be able to see him.

"I'm looking for a Wonder," he said, eyes flicking to the signs posted on the walls.

"The Song of the Sea." She lowered her voice, leaning over the bar so no one could overhear what she had to say. He met her eyes. Something about the way she knew what he was seeking made him think she was more than just a barmaid. "They say the last Siren is the key."

"To what?" Nikolai humored her, a playfulness in his otherwise tired voice. A glimmer of a smile appeared on his lips.

"Balance."

"I do not believe in prophecies and legends."

She reached over the bar and pressed her finger to his chest. "Balance within yourself."

"May I ask you something?" Nikolai asked, cutting her off. "Does Zidler remain in K'via?"

"Ah, yes. He does, he does. A half-hour walk from here." She nodded, a flash of knowing flickering in her smirk. "Why do you seek her?"

Thrown off by the sudden change in her expression, a grim look crossed Nikolai's face. Unsure how to properly answer that question, he repeated her words. "Balance."

"Good," she replied with a smile that creased the skin around her eyes.

"What is your name?" he asked.

The woman grinned before handing Nikolai his ale. "Otávia. Now, drink up, Nikolai. Be quick and find what you seek."

He opened his mouth to ask how she knew his name, but she disappeared behind the cellar doors, leaving him to his troublesome thoughts. Nikolai gripped his ale, the condensation dampening his fingertips. It was a very strong dark ale, just what he needed to calm his nerves. He was so close to the Siren. Slamming back the rest of the drink, he paid for it and disappeared with only a bad feeling about what he was going to do.

While the show's location was still undisclosed, Nikolai guessed it would be in an open field, close enough to the city that it would draw enough folk for Zidler to make a profit. Otávia told him it was a half hour away, which narrowed it down enough for him to confidently surmise the location. Tonight, he was going to retrieve the Siren. He could waste no more time.

Back at the carriage, he paused only to pet Kashmir behind the ears before preparing everything that he would need. A giant box full of seawater for the Siren, food for both Kashmir and her, gunpowder. Canisters of oil clinked together as he fumbled through them. When everything he needed was in the carriage, he brought it to the edge of the circus, just out of sight but close enough that he could reach it before being caught. Carrying the Siren would be the hardest part.

It was nearly midnight when Nikolai arrived. Giant striped tents of bright yellows and oranges spread before him. Lights flickered within them—Zidler was probably counting his income for the night. Trampled grass underfoot showed that a fair amount of people came from all around K'via to see the new Wonder.

His boots were filthy by the time he scouted the tents, trying to figure out which one held the Siren. Hidden off to the side, he watched for any sign to tell him which tent she was hidden within.

When he spotted two men even larger than him—brutes that were clearly the muscle of the show to keep too-eager people back from the Wonders—he knew where she was. Silent as a cat, Nikolai wove through the tents, scanning all around him as he approached. One mistake and he would be caught, probably beaten to death. The big man guarding the tent was watching for those who might enter through the front, so he pulled a metal peg from the ground and slipped under the canvas through the back.

The sight before his eyes made Nikolai pause, shaking him to his core. The smell of rancid blood made the hair on his neck stand on end. He grimaced, forcing himself to overcome the scent, and focused on the sight before him. The Siren was strung up, her hands over her head, tied with a rope that cut into her wrists. The meaty weight of her tail pulled her down, and it was clear to Nikolai that her shoulders were dislocated. In a worse state than he thought to see this soon into her capture, he felt immense guilt for allowing her to be in danger for this long. He should have killed everyone aboard that ship and let her go right then and there.

He added that to his ever-growing list of regrets.

Walking towards her, he could see the blood dripping from her body from gaping wounds spread across her back. She was now covered in black blood, dried and crusted in some places so it looked like tar. The fresher blood looked like the night sky in liquid form, without the beauty of the stars. He reached his hand up and placed it upon her cheek, then slid it down to her neck. She still had a pulse; he felt it faintly under his two fingers.

His touch caused her to stir; her amber eyes flickered before fully opening. She stared at him for a moment before realizing who she was seeing. Terror flashed across her eyes, and she tried to recoil, forgetting that she was tied up. When the binds sliced into her wrists further, she cried out. It was a guttural, throaty sound, dehydration cracking her voice.

Nikolai quickly covered her mouth. Tears slid down her cheeks and dampened his hand, and slowly, he pulled his hand away, placing his finger to his lips.

"I am not here to hurt you," he whispered. "I need you to stay as quiet as possible. Do you understand?"

She nodded gingerly, and Nikolai went to work. Reaching over her head, he began to cut at the ropes with a knife. As they slowly gave way, the Siren began to slip free of the bindings. He wrapped an arm around her waist before she fell, supporting her weight as best as he could before lowering her to the ground. Pulling the gunpowder from his bag, he spread it around the edges of the bright-colored canvas. Reaching for the lantern, he set it beside the edge of the tent where he had entered.

"I'm going to push you underneath the tent to the other side. Stay quiet and still," he told her.

The gap in the tent wasn't enough room for her to fit through, so he cut the thick fabric to give them more space. She still ended up smeared in mud, torn-up grass, and her own blood, but she made it to the other side.

Alone in the tent, Nikolai dumped the contents of the lantern out and watched as the gunpowder, canvas, and ropes burst into flame.

Nikolai left the burning tent and lifted the Siren into his arms. She weighed a ton, her tail almost double the length of her torso and heavy with muscle. He was unable to run as fast as he would have liked, but they made it a good distance before he heard shouting in his direction. She appeared terrified of everything.

Nikolai whistled loudly, and Kashmir came out of the darkness. The dog whipped past them and began to attack their pursuers. The screaming behind them made Nikolai grin. He listened keenly for any yelping, for he would always go back to save Kashmir, no matter what.

At the carriage, he slipped her into the box, saying, "It's temporary, I promise."

When he closed the lid, he watched her forlorn look turn to disgust. One cage to the next; why would she believe that he wasn't like the others? Casting aside the feeling of shame—he would have time to explain himself later—he shut the carriage door and whistled again. Within a minute, Kashmir was at his heels, then jumped up into the seat beside Nikolai. Blood dripped from Kashmir's jaws. Nikolai knew it was not Kashmir's blood by scent, and he took that as his cue to leave. The horses ran from the fiery catastrophe behind them into the safety of the night.

11

INTERLUDE

A six-year silence hung over the castle.

There was not a ripple in the heavy curtains, no windows were open, and all the sills were coated with gray dust. Cobwebs decorated every corner and every chandelier, their inhabitants catching the flies that dared enter the royal castle. The gray throne room was dark, the curtains shut, with only the occasional torch to light the way. What was once a place of beauty and splendor, with balls and festivities beyond the imagination of the common citizen, had fallen quiet and dark when there were no more Sirens.

All that was left were the echoes of their screams and the man who caused them.

A young soldier rushed down the hallway, his light footfall breaking the silence. He moved swiftly through the familiar halls and then turned down towards the royal corridor to find King Eiríkur. The Mad King.

Some say he was turned mad by all the Siren flesh he consumed. That their black blood poisoned his mind, or else he was cursed by a Sea Witch. Those who still lived in the castle knew he was mad, yes, but would rise again when he was told the words he had been waiting six years to hear.

Tentatively knocking upon the large oak door, the soldier waited. His nervousness rippled through him. Any time that the King was addressed face to face, the outcome was unpredictable. His temper sometimes led to the death of the messenger. Unless they brought good news.

The nurse whom the soldier was spending nights with answered the door, and they both blushed.

"I must speak with the King," he announced, quickly composing himself.

"He is not well."

"He will be."

She looked over her shoulder, then beckoned him in. The room smelled of sickness and age. Lifting her skirt, she moved out of the way, allowing the soldier to pass through. It was a well-known rule that no employee of the King was allowed to have any sort of relationship, physical or emotional. If he could not have what he wanted, neither could anyone else.

"King Eiríkur, the soldier has something to lift your spirits," she whispered gently as she poured him a cup of water.

He reached for the water, sipped it, then cleared his phlegm-filled throat. "What must you burden me with at this hour?"

"My King, a man has arrived with word of a Siren," the soldier told him.

"Come again, boy?" Eiríkur's eyebrow shot up. He was once the young prince who married the Queen of the Sea in his late thirties. Now, he had seen over sixty winters, and it showed.

"A...man has come from the harbor to inform you."

"Send him in."

Within a few minutes, a slender, gangly man stood politely at the bedside of the Mad King. "It is an honor to be graced by your presence," he said with a touch of sarcasm that the soldier heard, but Eiríkur did not. His accent hid it just enough. "My name is Vlad, your Majesty."

Vlad grinned, showing his teeth. The hair on the soldier's body stood entirely on end as he realized what sort of creature stood next to him.

"Why have you come?" Eiríkur demanded.

"A famous circus ringleader, Arthur Zidler, purchased a Siren from the Black Market not a week ago," he explained, his hands tucked neatly together in front of his body. "His show was burned to the ground, many of his creatures with it. He revealed he knew who it was, but he could offer no name and only a generic description of the criminal."

"And?" Eiríkur shouted.

"I happen to know who it is."

"Who? Tell me, or I shall have your head!"

Vlad grinned, wild eyes staring the Mad King down. "I need a promise."

"You can have as much gold as you want. I do not care."

"I have no use for gold." Vlad sneered, then composed himself. "The man who has this Siren—I want him."

The Mad King pondered the idea, stroking his wrinkled face. His dull blue eyes glanced at the Vampire. He spoke firmly. "Do what you want with him, but lay not a hand on the Siren."

"A Vampire does not break a promise," Vlad told him. "I only wanted the man, or rather, the Nightwalker, at the end of this. My employer asks for nothing more."

"Go, find me the Siren," Eiríkur told Vlad and the young soldier.

The hunt was on.

12

NIKOLAI

Ancient and neglected, falling apart in places, the only safe place Nikolai knew came into view. Faded white with paint that chipped away years ago, it appeared abandoned. It did not stand out in any way from other houses in the region—a simple slanted-roof home, a few windows that were curtained and some boarded up, and back doors just large enough for the Siren to fit through, with stables and a barn beside the house. Nikolai purchased the home many years ago; it had always been safe for him to visit every so often.

They arrived at the safe house before sunrise, though he cut it close. A raven quorked in the skies around them. Opening the double doors, wide enough to get the Siren inside, he pulled the carriage up to the porch. It was high enough that moving the glass box was not too difficult a task. When he yanked open the carriage doors, the Siren cringed at the lantern light. The one he put in the back of the carriage for her comfort went out at some point, and Nikolai felt a rush of guilt.

With the sun soon rising, he had no time to explain, so he carefully began to slide the box out of the carriage and onto the porch. The wood groaned underneath its weight, and Nikolai's muscles flexed, veins protruding from his skin as he pulled. The leather handles stretched but held the weight. Once they were inside, Nikolai cast a sorry glance at her. He would have to explain everything once he had confirmed they were safe. No one would have been able to follow, not when the chaos of the fire had distracted Zidler's men. Kashmir had handled anyone that dared pursue and deserved plenty of attention—that too would have to come later.

Nikolai brought everything into the house from the back of the carriage, placing odds and ends around the tank. When he had unloaded, he shut the house doors and took the carriage around to the side of the house. He made it inside just as the sun appeared over the horizon.

He shut the front door and glanced around the pure darkness of his safe house. He took a deep breath, telling himself that he survived the hardest part, though he knew there would be many more obstacles ahead. They were safe here for a few days, at least. The windows throughout the house were boarded up to prevent light from coming in, and rocky hills around the house obscured it from prying eyes. It was the only place Nikolai ever truly relaxed.

But there was no time to relax just yet. He lit all the lanterns and started a fire, which Kashmir lay in front of, sighing. It was clear the dog wanted to sleep but kept one eye open, watching Nikolai. Petting Kashmir's velvet coat, Nikolai checked him for any wounds. Kashmir shut his eyes, leaving him to tend to other matters.

In her glass cage, the Siren stared, laying horizontally with trauma all over her body and her blood staining the water. Nikolai crouched in front of the cage, then began to unlatch the top. He'd kept it locked to prevent her from escaping and getting herself caught all over again. Now, he needed to make her trust him, which he hoped would not be as difficult as it seemed. When the lid was opened, she attempted to shift so that her upper half was out of the box, but without her arms, it proved near impossible. Instead, she leaned her head over the edge, still far away from Nikolai. Her chest rose and fell heavily. They stared at one another.

"You're safe for now," he told her quietly.

She blinked.

"You do not speak?"

She shook her head.

He sighed. "But you understand what I am saying."

She hesitated, then nodded.

"May I tend to your wounds?" Nikolai gestured to her wounds.

A broken look crossed her face, contorting her beautiful features into something that saddened Nikolai. He understood the look, and so he rose to his feet to find alcohol, bandages, and a needle and thread; she was going to need a lot of care if she were to avoid infection. Arms full, Nikolai returned to the edge of the glass. Glancing at the tank, he wished he had something better to offer her. Aside from an unused and cobweb-filled claw foot tub, there was nothing else.

"I have to pop your shoulders back in place. It's going to hurt more than anything you've experienced."

Despair crossed her face.

"The pain will subside, and you will have use of your arms again."

She nodded slowly.

Nikolai kicked off his shoes, threw his jacket aside, then stepped barefoot into the box. Facing her, he gently touched her arm. It was smooth and clammy, as all Siren flesh was. Grabbing her upper bicep and elbow, he guided her arm back into the socket. She opened her mouth and cried out in pain, giving Nikolai a sense of what her voice might sound like. It would be a voice that could serenade anyone had it not been in such agony.

The bone popped back into place, and her eyes nearly bugged out of their sockets. She glanced furtively at her other arm; this one had an older wound that looked on the cusp of infection. They repeated the process without complication, and Nikolai stepped out of the box, splashing water all over the floor.

"I should explain." He opened a bottle of vodka and poured some onto a clean rag. Taking a swig from the bottle, he allowed the sharp taste and scent of the alcohol to overpower his senses and divert his attention away from her blood. "You are not my prisoner, and I do not intend to have you here for long."

She glanced over her shoulder, at him first and then the rag. She grimaced, recoiling. He wondered if she'd been put under chloroform before and if that was the reason behind her apprehension.

"We do have to lay low for some time to ensure no one knows where we have gone. Once the initial hunt has died down, we will get back on the road," he continued, applying some of the clear liquid to her back and her arm.

She did not cry out, but he saw her body tense.

"It will be a long, hard journey. There will be many people after me and even more after you. I will do everything in my power to keep you alive." Nikolai put the bottle and rag down and began to thread the needle. She had ten gaping cuts on her back that stretched over her width. Carefully, he began to sew up her back. One by one, he stitched the wounds.

He had stopped speaking while he sewed to ensure precision. Finished and having cleaned the blood and mud from her body, he leaned back against the wall, his knees bent. Reaching for the bottle of vodka, he brought it to his lips. The burning filled him with warmth that not even the crackling fire managed to do. The Siren leaned over the edge of the glass box, arms crossed and her head resting on the backs of her hands. Her gaze bore into him, and her white-blonde hair hung over the glass. He wished that she could speak.

There was more to be said, but the sun had risen, and Nikolai needed rest. After a moment, he put the cap back on the bottle and ran his hands through his hair. A wash would do him well, and he would do just that once the sun set. He shakily rose to his feet, surprised with how much the spirit hit him.

"If you need anything, just shout..." he paused, realizing his mistake, "or bang on the glass."

She smiled a soft, faint smile, but it reached her big eyes.

In his room, Nikolai hung his jacket on the bedpost. His shirt followed, and he stepped out of his wet trousers. He barely managed to wipe the blood from his hands before exhaustion floored him. When he fell upon his bed, it enveloped him with its warm embrace. The sheets smelled dusty and unwashed, but he didn't care.

Silence hung in the giant house. However, he was soothed, knowing that he did something right, something to absolve him of the mistakes he had made in his life. Taking a deep, relaxing breath, he shut his eyes and willed himself to sleep. Kashmir did not join him as he usually did—the dog always slept beside him—and Nikolai wondered if he preferred the company of the nameless stranger in the living room.

13

ÆSA

Æsa slept through the day despite the small space and the throbbing agony in her back and shoulders. The blinds were shut tight, so she had no concept of day or night, but it gave the impression she was in the safety and depth of the Sea, where no sun was able to penetrate. Having no idea of time was normal for her. She slept when she was tired, following her body's instinct. The first time she defied instinct, she got herself captured, sold, tortured, and now stolen. She sank to the bottom of her cage and released a deep breath, letting the bubbles obscure her vision for a few seconds.

When the flurry of bubbles cleared, she had a visitor. Seated beside the glass was the four-legged creature that followed the man. It was a dark gray color, with darker stripes over its body and hints of burnt orange. Æsa surfaced and leaned over the edge of the glass, staring at the animal. The creature looked up at her with big eyes that looked innocent. Gingerly, Æsa reached her hand out and felt the animal. Fur softer than anything she'd ever felt warmed her, and she could feel every muscle in its shoulders and back.

"Traitor," the man's voice mumbled sleepily from the doorway. He yawned, stretching his arms over his head. He wore only trousers, revealing his muscular chest and arms to her. He had tattoos around his biceps on both arms, simple black lines. On his back were bold black markings, starting below his trousers and snaking up his back all the way up his neck. "That's Kashmir."

Kashmir. Æsa repeated the name in her head. She glanced curiously at the man, raising her eyebrows at him, then cocking her head to the side. Her tongue still felt numb, too big for her mouth, and she was afraid of what might happen should she finally speak.

"I'm Nikolai."

Nikolai. Æsa said it in her head. Nikolai and Kashmir, her saviors. She hoped.

"What should I call you?" He asked the question, but they both knew that she wouldn't answer. He sauntered through the room where the fire pumped out warmth all day. Still looking at Æsa, he said, "I'm going out for a few hours. Kashmir will be by your side. No one will find us, but should someone stumble upon the house, Kash will handle it."

Nikolai left Æsa alone, and she felt the cold of the lonely house wrap itself around her. Even though there was a giant fire close by, she did not feel warm inside. She had not moved in days, not true swimming. She was being denied her most natural activity. A Siren was not meant to be caged, hunted, or eaten.

Though Æsa did not know how long she had been away from the Sea, she felt it had been ripped out of her. All that connected her to the planet, this place she called home, she felt leave her body when she left the Sea. The implications of this did not have time to resonate with her until now that she had a calm moment. She laid back in the glass box and flopped the end of her tail over the edge. Her gills opened and closed, as she still had not gotten used to breathing through her mouth.

Nikolai, the strange man who did not seem like one at all, had once terrified Æsa. When she first laid eyes on him, watching his piercing ocean-blue eyes bore into her, she feared his intentions. What she had quickly learned was that humans had very little humanity, which further led Æsa to believe Nikolai was no Man. The way he moved, the way he spoke, the way he tended to her wounds—none of it seemed in character for Man. So she concluded that he was not one at all.

She wondered what had made her so terrified of him to begin with. On that ship, when she first saw him, he had a determined look. Now she knew that his goal was not to eat or torture or test her but to protect her, perhaps even save her life. She dared to let herself entertain the idea that maybe he would return her to the ocean. It was the only thing she hoped for, the only thing she would fight for. Æsa would choose death over anything she had been through since she reached the surface. Having not heeded the warnings of her dead Sisters, she put herself to shame in their shadows. They had died in vain.

Since Nikolai had saved her, she sensed something different in him. At first glance, he had a hard demeanor, a scowl almost permanently on his face. But when that scowl vanished, he was comely, with a face that could be striking. During the rescue, Æsa did not know what to expect once she was taken out from the back of the carriage, but Nikolai tending to her wounds was not an option that had crossed her mind. Reaching her webbed hands over her shoulders and wincing in pain, she fingered the perfect stitching on her back.

Something tickled her fins, and she recoiled just a bit, though she did not withdraw her tail. When her eyes landed on Kashmir, his long tongue licking the end of the fins, she smiled, then began to giggle. The animal glanced up, tongue halfway out of his mouth. A brief stare down, and then Æsa leaned forward, her arms extending so she was reaching over her tail. Her flesh upon her back stretched, and her shoulders cried out, but she urged herself through the pain. Petting Kashmir's floppy jowls, she grinned as the drool stuck to her hands. Such new feelings, new experiences—she had to savor the good among the bad.

She decided to try her words to see if she could remember how to speak. Staring at the dog in front of her, she said his name in her head over and over. *Kashmir. Kashmir. Kashmir.* It seemed so simple in her mind; how easy it would be to speak one simple word. Clearing her throat, Æsa formed her lips into a shape, her tongue pressing to the roof of her mouth. No, that was wrong. She put her tongue somewhere else, trying to relax it.

"Kos—"

She shook her head. "Kaass."

She growled in frustration.

"Kash-mir." She managed at last, then grinned as the dog perked his ears up. "Kash-mir."

Her first word in ten years was the name of a dog, and she could not have been happier.

14

NIKOLAI

Showing his face in K'via so soon after setting Zidler's circus on fire was a risk Nikolai had to take, so he slipped into an unfamiliar tavern to hear what people were saying. What he learned would help him decide what path to take, for the journey would be perilous. Seated at a table tucked in the far corner, he leaned back and listened to the patrons around him. Familiar and unfamiliar tongues spoke only of the great fire—there had not been this kind of talk since the Great Wars when the Mad King used all his power to find every Siren to devour. Nikolai had caused a rift in the balance, and he knew it would return to him tenfold. He had started something—something big.

A pair of men talked openly about the Sirens they ate in the past and how they would kill anyone to get their hands on the last Siren. They threw back ale and laughed about what horrible things they would do to keep her alive as long as they could to devour her slowly.

Clutching his drink in his hand, Nikolai fought the urge to stalk over there and drain them of their blood. He needed to be smart about his meals, particularly in the city. Flagging the barmaid down, he ordered two more ales to be brought to their table. When they were good and drunk, perhaps passed out in the alley behind the tavern, Nikolai would feed. Then, he could return to the safe house.

So long as he got the Siren to where she would be safe, Nikolai didn't care what happened to him then.

He had his brother sending his goons after him to return him to the Brotherhood, where he would be ridiculed, humiliated, beaten, tortured, and then maybe—if his brother felt kind—killed off at last. Killing a Vampire was not difficult; they were no different from humans despite the myths and rumors that had spread since the dawn of time. Crosses and stakes to the heart were among some of the theories. A stake to the heart would kill anyone.

Nikolai had been avoiding his brother for a long time, and nothing had changed since he decided to leave the Brotherhood ten years ago. Shaking the thought from his head, not wanting to think about his brother, he tried to drown himself in some ale. Something stronger could take the edge off, but he swore off any substance that wasn't liquor a long time ago. He owed it to the Siren to be in his right mind.

Contemplating the fact that Zidler would be after him, Nikolai suspected he would be an easier opponent than his brother. Zidler had his hand in many pockets, so finding the money to hire people to hunt Nikolai would not be difficult for the ringleader. Though he put on a show and a smile, he was a villain through and through. The state that the Siren was in showed Nikolai that. She had been in his clutches not even a fortnight, and she was half dead when he found her. He knew Zidler would do anything to get her back.

It would not surprise Nikolai if the presumed-dead King Eiríkur rose from the grave to hunt him down, too.

As if to confirm his suspicions, he overheard the words behind him.

"The army is rising," a man whispered coldly. "Silent for years, I saw soldiers marching through the city. Ransacking is beginning, so if you have anything to hide, best you rid yourself of it now."

Another man responded, "So Eiríkur is alive. I heard there is a Siren, the *last* one. It is the only thing that could rouse a dead king."

"A storm is coming," said the first man, "and blood is going to be spilled."

A bone-chilling voice rang through Nikolai's mind: *"Balance within yourself."*

Glancing around, Nikolai did not see the dark-skinned barmaid who had told him about the balance. He would have sworn he heard her voice, that thick accent and smooth like velvet voice. It was not to be mistaken, making him realize he had a run-in with a Witch.

Sighing, Nikolai pushed his half-empty pint away from him. As he leaned against the back of the chair, he rotated his shoulders to stretch, his mind drifting to the Siren. Despite all she had suffered, he could not promise her safety. By rescuing her, he had put her in danger. He had a target on his back, but that was a familiar thing for Nikolai. People were trying to kill him from all directions, but he still had a few friends.

His head spun slightly as he realized this was going to be the most difficult task of his life—and he had fought in a war. So many people were after him, and even more were after the Siren. A Witch knew what he was, who he was, and what he was doing. The only thing he didn't have after him was a Werewolf, though he wouldn't be surprised if someone decided to send one after him; the Witch Roman had at his side was a Luca, after all. He shook the thought from his head. He was safe from that, at least—that Wolf could not cross borders.

Nevertheless, he needed to move the Siren and fast.

Slowly, Nikolai rose from his wooden seat and decided to find a meal, then get back home as soon as possible. Too many people already knew of the Siren, thanks to Zidler and his big mouth. It would not be long before his safe house was no longer safe.

"Balance within yourself, Nikolai." Her voice was relentless, throbbing in his head like a dozen wasps trying to escape his skull.

One of the men Nikolai ordered ale for stepped out of the tavern. Nikolai followed him. To no surprise, the drunken man collapsed against the wall of the building. Sometimes, Man made it too easy. He didn't mind the hunt, after all—it was in his nature—but some nights it was a nice surprise to find someone who wouldn't put up a fight. The body would be found in the morning, just another man who drank himself to death. Nikolai made quick work of the man and fed with vigor.

In an almost drunken state himself, he made it back to the safe house without any complications aside from the Witch's voice ringing inside of his head. He did not know what sort of balance he was seeking or even what it meant to have balance. Shaking the thoughts from his head, he stepped into the house and felt eyes on him immediately. When he glanced at the Siren, wishing that he at least knew her name, he offered her the closest thing to a smile that he could.

Walking past her, he fed the fire with a few logs, then collapsed into a large chair. Hands resting on the arms, he began to pick at the loose threads. Her eyes were still on him, and he could not resist looking at her. When he glanced up and met her gaze, he saw that she was smiling.

"What do you have to smile about?" he asked.

She cocked her head to the side, her tongue darting out to dampen her lips before she blushed, shying away. Nikolai noted that while she still looked like she had been beaten half to death, she looked healthier. Maybe it was the smile.

"We'll move in a few days time. We cannot stay here." He sighed, glancing at the blacked-out window. "The journey will be hard, and I do not have anything more comfortable for transporting you. But I will get you to a safe place."

She responded with a nod. She beckoned him closer then, a simple wave of her webbed hand. Nikolai felt unable to disobey her command, as if the stories he was told as a child were true, and Sirens lured men to their demise. Rising from his chair, he knelt by the edge of her glass box. She reached out and grabbed his wrapped hands. Slowly, she began to unwrap the bandages. Her fingers were clammy as they gently peeled back the cloth. When they were exposed, he remained still while she looked over his cut hands. Bruises that extended down the length of the back of his hand, knuckles cut with blood and dirt smeared over them.

"Some people believe that a Siren's kiss can heal people. That their kiss can heal all wounds, diseases, and ailments," he told her, though he did not believe it. It was something his brother would have believed, but not him.

Sirens and Vampires didn't have powers; they just had problems.

"My brother believes in all of that," he added quietly.

She narrowed her eyes and moved her hand to the back of his head. The water sloshed out of the box as she moved, pulling her upper half out of the box, one hand on the edge of it to hold her up. Her hand felt so strange on the back of his neck but soothing too. Half of him expected her to break his neck, though he knew she did not have the strength to do that. The other half of him expected her to kiss him, yet he was still surprised when she did. Her color-drained lips pressed against his, and he was so startled by the salty kiss that he did not kiss her back.

When she pulled away, she dipped her head down but kept her eyes peering up at him through loose blonde locks. Her tongue pressed against her own canine before darting back inside her mouth. Her eyes told him that she was proving that they had no powers, nothing special about them. Her kiss would do nothing for anyone—it would cure no ailments and save no lives.

Nikolai pressed his fingers to his lips, the phantom of her kiss still lingering.

Then she reached her hand up and lifted his lip, exposing his fangs. Studying them, she narrowed her amber eyes into slits. Nikolai didn't move, shocked but intrigued by her strange behavior. Part of him believed it was her opening up to him, the early stages of trust developing. Slowly, she released him and bent her head to the side.

"You are...not Man," she spoke so softly that Nikolai thought he imagined it. "Not really."

"I'm not? What makes Man?"

"Greed," she whispered.

15

ÆSA

Being so close to Nikolai made Æsa feel safe now. Staring at him so close to her, their lips having touched moments ago, she wondered what made her so terrified when she first saw him. He had eyes of the Sea, and she could stare into them for days should she be given the opportunity. But within those bright eyes, there was so much darkness. Knowing how horrible the past could be, she wondered what his life had been like and how he ended up here saving a Siren from a life of torture and likely a slow, painful death.

"So, now that you are done giving me the silent treatment," he said with an eyebrow arched, "may I have your name?"

She had not said her name in so many years, but it rolled off her tongue smoothly. "Æsa."

"Æsa," he repeated, pronouncing it perfectly; with his accent, it sounded even more beautiful. He flashed a grin, teeth on full display. "Well, Æsa, if you have any questions, now is the time to ask. I'm somewhat intoxicated and willing to spill my secrets."

Her light hair fell over her shoulder, the wet waves cascading over her breasts. When she brushed it back so that it was all clumped together and now draping down her back, she noticed Nikolai's eyes flicker down briefly, then back up to her eyes. When they held each other's gaze, there was no shame in his eyes. Sirens did not wear clothing —they were natural to their surroundings like all the other creatures of the Sea and the Land. Only Man covered up who they were with clothing and lies.

"If you are not Man, what are you?" she asked quickly but carefully.

Nikolai leaned back, sitting with his knees propped up before him. He draped his arms around his legs and clasped his hands together. His eyes seemed to look through her as he debated how to answer her question. When his striking gaze focused back on her, a faint smile dusted his pale lips.

"I am..." he paused, "an outcast, a hunter, and the hunted. I am not a good person, and I will never have clean hands."

As if to prove a point, he raised his bloodied hands once again. The days-old wounds tried to scab over, but blood still seeped from them. Covered in blood and scratches was the faded gray tattoo of a flower.

Æsa studied Nikolai, trying to make sense of him and his words. He offered himself up as an open book, yet when Æsa questioned him about what he was, he had not truly answered. Perhaps the answer made sense to him—it was what he believed himself to be—but Æsa was still confused. Confused about what he was, why he had saved her, why he wanted to protect her. So, she decided to press further. "You have done... bad things?"

"Absolutely," he answered.

She nodded, then asked, "Then why did you rescue me?"

He glanced at the windows, black and empty, then back into her full-of-life eyes. "Where I come from, it is rumored that Sirens are the spirits of women who were murdered, particularly drowned. I know this is not true, yet whenever I heard of another murdered for Man's hunger, I thought of my mother."

"What happened to your mother?"

"Æsa, I am a Vampire," he said outright. "Do you know what that is?"

She shook her head.

"Vampires need to feed on human blood to live."

"Is this why you think you are bad?"

"No." He showed no guilt for what he had to eat to survive. "There are two ways of becoming a Vampire: being born as one and being turned by the bite of one.

"Those who are born as Vampires often see themselves as pure-blooded. Not tainted by the very thing they feast upon, never having once been their own food source." Nikolai went into the explanation, leading Æsa closer to the truth. "While Man and Siren had their wars, Vampires went to war with each other in my country. Pure Blood versus Half-Blood. They fought until a balance was met. There were many, many casualties."

"Your mother?" Æsa asked.

He nodded. "I have two brothers, both older. They were turned from human to Vampire by our father. He himself had been turned after their human birth. Once my father was made into a Vampire, he saw all humans as food, including my mother and brothers. To protect them, my mother begged him to turn the whole family. And so, I became the first and last Pure-Blood Sokolov."

"They envied you," Æsa figured out.

"It was more than envy." Nikolai's voice had a tone of despair. "At first, they promised me everything I wished for. I was young and impression-able, and I wanted something to fight for. Their fight seemed as good as any. Later, I realized that they gave me these false promises to keep me compliant. I did their bidding without question. I killed anyone who dared mention my brothers' impure blood. Over the years, we became known as the Brotherhood, and soon the wars came to an end. We proved that Pure Bloods and Half Bloods could live together in harmony. Vampires from around Osleka envied us, envied the power we had taken. My older brother Roman built himself a throne and called himself *Korol*."

"What happened to your mother?" Æsa repeated her question from before.

Nikolai sighed. "I left the Brotherhood to return home after my father died. I did not care for the politics and the lies, and I did not care for my brother putting himself above us all. Some of the things he made me do..." he trailed off. "I did not want to take it from him—his Brother-hood—he *had* done a lot of good. So, I left instead of causing trouble. I lived at home for some time, as normal a life as a Nightwalker can—"

"Nightwalker?"

"Another name for what I am. Vampires cannot survive in the sun."

Æsa's eyes glanced around at all the blacked-out windows and understood.

Nikolai continued. "The thing about Pure Bloods is that we have natural authority and strength, like Alphas in a Wolfpack. Without my presence in the Brotherhood, the others began to question if the Brotherhood was actually about equality among all Vampires when only two Half Bloods sat upon the thrones.

"Roman asked me to return, to keep the balance. Which, to him, meant killing anyone who questioned us. I did not wish to return, all I wanted was a life of peace—or one as peaceful as possible when my food source meant killing Man. Another thing that separated Roman and I was that he kept humans as a constant source of food. I, on the other hand, select my food carefully. The sick, the dying, the abusers, the cruel, and those who wished to die.

"One evening I returned home to find Roman and Ivan, my other brother..." Nikolai shuddered. "They had returned home. Immediately I knew something was wrong, I did not have to ask them what they had done. There was a lake behind the house, and I saw her immediately—my mother, face down with her white dress splayed all around her like a water lily. They drowned her so that I would return to the Brotherhood —so that I would have no other family in the world but them. Roman killed everyone I've ever loved. My mother, my best friend, my lover..."

"You think your mother became a Siren?" Æsa's voice was a whisper. She knew it could not be true, for if every woman who drowned became like her, she would not have been alone so long.

"I know she didn't. Death is death. It is final. I have seen enough of it to know," he told her. "But when I heard of the hunt for Sirens for food, I couldn't help but feel the need to protect them. To protect you."

16

NIKOLAI

The few days and nights that they remained in the safe house went by fast. As Æsa healed, Nikolai noticed her relative comfort in his home. They slept throughout the day, Æsa adapting quickly to Nikolai's schedule. Twice, he moved her from the cage to the large bathtub to swap out the water. Nikolai sensed they were both desperate for a bond as they had been alone for so long. With every smile she gave him, a connection developed between them. Over the days they were around one another, they quickly built trust.

"We'll leave at dusk tonight," Nikolai told her after waking.

Æsa was currently in the bathtub, her tail hanging over the edge. She leaned back against the curve of the metal, her arms resting on either side of the tub. Her hair hung behind her, nearly touching the ground in long, white waves. Nikolai had cleaned the glass cage, ensuring it would be fit for travel as he was unsure when they would get another break. He had very few acquaintances along the way whom he could trust. The journey across the country was difficult, the terrain unforgiving, and having someone to house them for even a few days to recoup later in the trek was necessary.

"Nikolai," Æsa's voice chimed from the bathroom, and when he entered, he couldn't help but catch a glimpse at her exposed breasts. It had been a long time since he had last seen a Siren, and he sometimes forgot how little they cared about nudity. She brought her hand to her lips and cocked her head to the side. "May I ask one thing of you?"

"Of course." He was about to take her across Kæ'vale with a good chance he'd get her killed along the way: he would grant her anything in his power.

"I feel like I am being..." she paused and searched for the word, "suffocated, unable to move, unable to swim."

"You want me to stop somewhere?" he asked. "I cannot go to the ocean; they'll be scouring the shores for you. Fresh water is the best I can do."

"Fresh water?" She furrowed her brows.

"A lake—no salt. Don't worry. Your kind can be in either."

She nodded. "I just need to move."

"I will do the best that I can," Nikolai promised.

"That is all I can ask of you," she said, her eyes placid. "Is it wrong to be scared?"

"I would be concerned if you weren't," Nikolai admitted.

Dusk consumed the northern hemisphere, the dark skies revealing stars that glittered in the distance. The greens of the fields turned into a blend of browns and shades of gray, melding with the sky. For a time, there was no telling the difference between land and sky, but Nikolai saw well in the dark. With Æsa in the back, sloshing around in that horrid cage that made his guilt a constant companion, he had to move carefully. The horses led the carriage down the path away from the safe house, moving as though they knew exactly where they were going.

Through the small window, he could look in the back and see Æsa and Kashmir. Nikolai left the lid to her cage open, but had explained to her that if they stopped suddenly or he knocked twice on the wood of the carriage, she was to close it. A blanket was attached to the lid so that she and the cage would be covered from anyone who glanced in. All they would see was Kashmir, who was lying comfortably with his tongue sloppily out of his mouth. If they dared look further, Kashmir would attack.

The horses plodded on, stopping at Nikolai's command as the carriage got caught on a rock here and there, detouring when they ran into impassable crevices. They made a good distance before Nikolai took a small detour and found a small lake, barely more than a pond. It was crystal clear, and some ice had formed around the edges, but it would have to do. The moon was still out when they arrived, so when Nikolai opened the back of the carriage, Æsa got a real chance to see the night sky, pausing to stare at the brilliant colors of green and blue shimmering across its expanse.

Nikolai beckoned for her to come closer, his arms out so he could carry her over to the water, but she was frozen solid like a statue. Noticing her amazement, he grunted his understanding. "Where I come from, we call it Nightsun. It's not common to see it this late in the year."

"It is the most beautiful thing I have ever seen," she marveled. She caught sight of the dark water in front of her. Her eyes grew wide with longing.

She heaved her body out of the box, and Nikolai assisted, carrying her the short distance to the pond. She pushed herself out of his grasp once he was knee-deep. He stood there a moment, watching her disappear beneath the placid surface. The ripples caused by her body shimmered and distorted the reflection of the night sky above them.

Æsa dove deep and was gone from his sight. Nikolai watched as the water rippled outwards, then went placid again. He knew she would be disappointed when she realized how shallow fresh water was, but he hoped it was enough for her to feel alive again.

He emerged from the water, not minding the wetness of his shoes and trousers. Nikolai sat at the edge of the carriage, allowing her the time to swim. Drawing the map from his bag, he traced his finger over the path they needed to take, the towns they would have to go through, the ones they could skirt around. His eyes were drawn to the pond, thinking about the vulnerable life out there.

Sirens weren't meant to be on Land or in ponds.

Moments later, she surfaced with a faint smile on her lips. Nikolai sat on the edge of the carriage, hand upon Kashmir's head and his eyes on the brilliant sky where a large bird circled lazily—odd for this time of night. When he looked at Æsa, she blushed, lowering herself into the waters so that only the pierced bridge of her nose and higher were above the surface. Her hands waved in and out around her.

"I'll try to do this as often as possible, but I cannot promise you it will be easy," he said to break the tension. The way she looked at him made him ache in a way he didn't know was possible. His ability to trust had been damaged when his mother was murdered by her own sons, but even before that, he did not stay connected to any one person for very long. If his brothers taught him one thing, it was to never care for anything. They would always take it from him.

Æsa raised herself so that her shoulders were exposed to the sharp air. "How long is the journey going to be?"

"About a month...should all go well." His statement reminded Æsa that not everything would go well or according to plan. It never did.

Nikolai noticed Kashmir perk up, his ears pointed straight upwards, tail between his muscular legs. His guard went up, hair rising on the back of his neck. Creeping forward, the dog jumped out of the carriage with Nikolai close behind. Eyes scanning, he peered at Æsa long enough to put his finger to his lips, then gestured with a lowering hand, palm down, telling her that she should submerge herself.

Three men emerged, cresting the hill above where they waited. They were clad in well-maintained garb. The men knew what they were after, but Nikolai did not know who sent them. He wondered who was paying them, as he had no doubt there was a bounty on his head now. The men and Vampires that Roman had sent after him had been scraggly at best, but perhaps he had grown tired of waiting on men who could not defeat Nikolai and had sent in better people. Two pursued Nikolai, the third going straight to the water's edge. Nikolai's lip raised.

"Kash." Nikolai only needed to speak his name before the dog prowled along the shore, cutting off the man before he could enter the water where Æsa hid.

A hefty bark echoed over the water, and Kashmir lunged at the man. Sharp teeth sank into the man's arm, but he wore protective gear. He shook the dog, but Kashmir hung on, dragging him down with his weight. Once Kashmir began to back up, the man went down, fighting against the tug of the large dog.

Nikolai, facing both men, raised both his eyebrows quickly. "Two against one isn't very fair, now is it?"

"Lucky for us, we caught wind of your reputation." One of the men grinned, hands raised to his chin in a fighting stance. The other appeared over-confident, hands clenching and unclenching by his side, his anger-fueled expression making his bearded face red.

"Then you'll know these situations tend to go in my favor." Nikolai playfully beckoned them forward, challenging them. If there was one thing an over-confident man could not turn away from, it was another man challenging him.

The moment the bearded man closed in on him, Nikolai took advantage of the fact he did not protect his face with his fists. A swift uppercut sent him stumbling back, shouting and clutching his newly broken nose. His hands held his face, blood gushing through his fingers. Human— Nikolai could smell every drop.

Clearly more experienced than the bearded man, the other came at Nikolai with quick feet, jabbing his arm out and catching Nikolai in the wrist. Nikolai shoved his hand back and brought his leg up to kick his opponent right to the stomach. His foot forced the man back, but he regained his stance quickly and threw a handful of punches. Left and right, back and forth, they danced. The bearded man recovered to the best of his ability, ignoring the blood streaming down his face, and pursued Nikolai with more rage in his movements.

Nikolai glanced up momentarily to check on Kashmir and Æsa. She was still under the water, and Kashmir appeared to be handling his own opponent quite well. He had dragged the man down to the muddy shores of the lake, biting down on his exposed throat and gnawing away like he was a chew toy. Muscles flexing and jaws snapping, the dog relentlessly tore the windpipe, the man's shouting turning to gurgles, then nothing at all. When the dog sensed the man was dead, he dashed off to assist Nikolai. He lunged at the bearded man, but he kicked Kashmir before he was able to snap down his jaw.

The dog whimpered but was not put off by the new opponent. Nikolai, however, heard the yelp and glanced over to ensure that his best friend was okay. The two-second distraction earned Nikolai a solid punch to the jaw, and he stumbled backward. Gripping his sore jaw, he grinned at the man who punched him, adrenaline fueling him. With an unexpected sweep of his leg, he got the man on the ground, but instead of pummeling him like he planned to, Nikolai felt the overwhelming desire to devour. The scent of blood all around him distracted him more than he realized, and so, putting his trust in Kashmir to watch his back, he sank his teeth into the man's throat before he could even scream.

17

ÆSA

When Nikolai signaled for Æsa to hide, she knew it was too late. The men had spotted her, and she was certain they knew of her presence before they revealed themselves. Still, she pushed back from the shore and disappeared below the surface.

Being defenseless infuriated her; her nails dug into her palms as her strong tail pushed her deeper down. If Nikolai and Kashmir did not survive this, there was only so much she could do. Waiting the men out would be impossible—there was nothing she could live off of in this lake. They would come for her. Æsa swam to the far edges of the lake and popped her head up. She had to know what was happening. Waiting for Nikolai to fight for her life, as well as his own and Kashmir's, was agonizing.

It was too much like her Sisters all fighting to save her. Dying to keep her alive.

Scanning the scene before her, she saw Nikolai ripping out the throat of one man. Another lay dead on the shore, his blood seeping into the waters and tainting them. Kashmir lunged at the only man left alive, but the man kicked him. He began walking towards the water, but Kashmir ran to stop him.

The bearded man gave Kashmir another kick, but the dog was able to dart away in time. This gave the man the opening he needed, and he sprinted to the water, aiming for Æsa. Kashmir pursued, but once at chest height in the water, the dog knew he was unable to fight, so he began to bark.

Æsa quickly submerged again, listening to every splash and knowing exactly where the man was. She was in her element and could feel every shift in the water. She waited for him to come to her.

The man threw his heavy jacket off, and it floated on the water like a corpse, empty and lifeless. Then he dove where he had last seen Æsa. There was little light aside from what the moon offered, but her bright tail was reflective of the moonlight, and she was easy to spot in the shallow lake. He did not know that she was waiting. He pushed his limits as he swam deeper but misjudged one thing.

No Man could outswim a Siren.

Æsa rose up to meet the man, his eyes boring into her, hunger within them. Blood streamed out of his nose, souring the water. He seemed amazed, stunned even, that she was swimming towards him, ignorant of the long-drawn death that he was going to receive.

Æsa raised her hands and met him in the water, pushing him up with the force of her body. The blow made him rise slightly, almost to the surface. Stunned by her show of force, he paused for a moment too long. She swirled in the water so she was above him. She used the power of her tail to push him down to the muddy floor of the lake. His hands grabbed at her, his body writhing in protest when he realized what was happening, but she had the upper hand. Baring her teeth, she hissed through the water until his back hit the bottom.

Æsa made sure her eyes were open to witness life leaving him. When his hands stopped fighting, his body no longer moving, she released him. She stared for a while, looking at the person she had murdered. There was no guilt within her.

She felt empowered.

"Æsa!" Nikolai's voice sounded muffled below the rippling water.

Æsa could hear his footfall in the lake, how his burly figure disrupted the water. She surfaced as quickly as she could, resulting in half of her body springing from the water, and then she sank back into her shoulders.

"I am here," she said.

"Are you okay?" Panic riddled his voice, denting his normally casual demeanor.

"Yes," she confirmed. "He is dead."

"Good, let's get you out of there." Nikolai waded a little further in, crouching down and putting his arms just under the water.

Æsa maneuvered so she was in his arms, and he lifted her. As he carried her back to the carriage, she reached up and touched her hand to his bruising jawline.

Nikolai grunted. "It's fine."

"You would go through all of this for me?" she asked.

His blue eyes met her amber ones. "What more must I go through to prove myself to you?"

She laughed as he slid her into the glass box, then leaned over the edge. "You have blood on your face."

"Saving it for later." His rarely seen grin was infectious, but he quickly turned to find Kashmir, and the smile disappeared. "Kash!"

The dog loped over, bruised like his owner.

"He is a very good friend," Æsa remarked.

"Man's best friend, that's what they say." Nikolai massaged the soft spot behind Kashmir's ears.

"But you are not Man."

"No."

He went to say more, but Æsa cut him off. "You are so much more."

Some nights later, crammed in the back of the carriage, Nikolai looked too large for the small space. He shifted uncomfortably every few minutes. Æsa suspected there was more to his discomfort than just the position he was in. Discomfort lingered beneath his skin, festering like a wound.

Æsa had her tail out of the box and leaned back with a kink in her neck that she never complained about. If she was on her way to freedom as Nikolai promised, she wasn't going to complain if she could help it. She gazed at him, watching as he tried to find a comfortable position, and wondered how many times he had done this before. Saved a Siren. He explained why he protected her kind, but she still didn't understand why he put himself at risk. Had he believed the story of drowned women becoming Sirens, it would have made sense, but Æsa still felt as though she was missing a piece of the puzzle. Something crucial, something that would explain his discomfort.

Holding her tongue, Æsa simply watched him with keen interest. Having been alone for so many years, she only ever saw the creatures of the Sea and the memories that flashed in her mind every time she went to sleep. Lately, those memories had not surfaced. She slept in darkness and peace each day when Nikolai was beside her, but he had not. Æsa had woken many times throughout the days, her slumber disrupted only by Nikolai speaking in his sleep, writhing and shaking the carriage.

When Nikolai seemingly found a comfortable position, Æsa asked, "Who were those men?"

Nikolai raised his pale eyebrows, then shrugged. "Could be anyone, really. Siren hunters, people after me, Zidler's hired muscle. It appeared they were after you, but they knew about me. It is impossible to say."

He flashed an unconvincing smile. He looked down at his hands, picking at a scab. Æsa used this moment to study his brokenness. His body was worn down, and he looked sallow despite his strength. For many nights, the journey had been tedious. While they had not run into anyone else since the men at the lake, each unaccounted-for stop, each detour over the rough terrain, each time Nikolai had to work the carriage wheels out of a rut, weathered him. She could do nothing to help, and her weight, plus the weight of the glass box, only added to the difficulty. Her body ached from being jostled around and holding herself steady, and she could only imagine how Nikolai felt.

"You're going hungry."

He nodded. "We will pass through a town when night falls. I'll get something for both of us there."

When night fell, Æsa woke to an empty carriage. She yawned, stretching her arms over her head as Nikolai opened the doors again. He did not stare like a young man might; he averted his eyes at her exposure.

"Good evening." Nikolai raised both eyebrows quickly. "You have to get dressed."

"What's 'dressed?'" She brought her arms back down and leaned over the box, her hair falling in front of her.

"Clothes, like the rest of us wear."

"No."

Nikolai laughed. "I can't go through the town with you in the back of the carriage. They are ransacking homes—I imagine they will be searching all carriages that go through. I'd go around, but it's impassable with the carriage. We'll have to stick to the road. And we have to get rid of the box."

"You realize I will die out of water?" she asked with an incredulous essence to her melodic voice.

"We'll have a few hours." Nikolai made a thoughtful face, a charming sort of sheepish smile. "I promise I'll make it up to you as soon as I'm able. We have to stick somewhat close to the shore for a while, which means more patrols. Of course, we will need a new tank for you, which means I have to stop somewhere..." he faltered for a moment. "I should be able to get you somewhere safe in a fortnight."

"And then?"

"You'll be free. In the ocean."

She beamed up at him. Just the thought of the icy saltwater touching her flesh made all the pain disappear. She felt nothing of the wound on her arm, which was all but healed now, the carnage of her back, or the fact she had barely had a chance to move and swim in days. Imagining the undercurrent gliding over her skin, she closed her eyes and breathed in the air around her. To be able to picture it again and knowing it was within her reach now, she knew she would do anything to get there.

Opening her eyes, she said, "So, these clothes..."

Nikolai smirked and rifled through a bag, pulling out a giant clump of fabric that Æsa thought might swallow her up. As he removed other garments from the bag, she quickly began to regret the decision to be clothed. Unable to move freely on land, she felt restricted from doing so. He laid the clothing out and then glanced at her almost nervously. "I need to get you out of the box, and you're going to have to practice sitting upright."

Æsa rolled her eyes, hoping Nikolai would not see, but he caught it and smirked. Laying down the clothing, he beckoned for her to come closer. Wrapping her arms around his neck, she clung tight while he slipped his hand underneath her tail and lifted her from the box. Sitting her on the edge of the carriage, he slowly released her while giving her tips on remaining seated. When he stepped back, she was wavering side to side but managed to stay upright. She flicked her eyes up to look at him and raised both eyebrows. "Sirens are able to sit, Nikolai."

He shrugged. "Typically, the ones who don't come to the surface don't get the hang of it so fast."

"You've done this before?" Now was her chance to pry.

He nodded, his expression pinched. He reached past Æsa to grab the clothing and held up a loose-fitting blouse.

She reached her hands up as she'd seen him do whenever he dressed, thinking about the dark markings upon his skin, the tattoos that she longed to get a better look at. The blouse was less uncomfortable than she expected, and she gave the okay for the skirt. It was more diffi-cult to get over her tail, but once it was on, it covered almost all of her long tail, but she had to curl it to hide the fins. Her gills would be covered by a scarf; her hands by gloves.

"How do I look?" she asked. "I feel ridiculous. How do people wear all this?"

"You look ridiculous." Nikolai grinned, flashing his teeth. "Now, let's get through this, shall we?"

She took a deep breath and nodded her head quickly, as though she'd never go through with this if she hesitated. Her life had flipped completely upside down since she reached the surface, and while she had more excitement in the last week or so that she'd been out of the water, the ache in her shoulders and the searing hot pain in her back reminded her of her mistakes.

But the ocean was not far now.

18

NIKOLAI

After Æsa was dressed, Nikolai propped her in the front of the carriage and told her to practice staying as still as possible, looking like a proper lady, and avoiding revealing her tail at all costs. From there, he left Kashmir to guard the carriage. Dragging the large tank, he pulled it along the dirt and grass until he reached a deep pond a hundred meters from the carriage. He was alert as he listened for any noises. Kashmir had a bark that could shake a man to his core, so he knew he would hear him should anything happen.

Without further delay, Nikolai pulled the tank into the pond and ensured it was submerged. His next planned destination was to acquire a new tank and have a few days rest crossed his mind. Traveling without a tank was possible, but since their encounter with the men at the lake previously, Nikolai didn't want to risk it. He was already vulnerable, having to hide out during the day, and if they didn't make it to a body of water by the time he was forced to stop, Æsa wouldn't survive. No, he needed a new tank, and he knew where he could go to get one.

On his return trip, he saw a flash of Æsa's near-white hair as she glanced to the right of the carriage. Relieved that she was still there and unharmed, he strolled a little more casually. Before now, he had been riding up front to control and guide the horses, usually alone as Kashmir had opted to lay next to Æsa. It was clear that the dog also cared about her and felt the same need to protect her. That, or he was in tune enough to Nikolai's feelings that he wanted to protect her for his owner. Nikolai smiled at the thought, seeing both Æsa and Kashmir up front next to his seat. It was almost reminiscent of family.

He suddenly felt as though they would get through this.

Because if they didn't, Nikolai didn't know what he would do.

Without interruption, it would only take them an hour to get through the town. Any delay would leave Æsa suffering in great agony. A Siren could last nearly a day out of the water; less if the sun was present. But the pain set in after only a few hours. Any longer and she would go into a catatonic state before she died. Those who nearly perished before explained that it felt like dying of thirst or lack of oxygen. There had been many rich Siren collectors who performed tests on them; Nikolai had seen more than his fair share since he arrived in Kæ'vale.

"Kash," Nikolai called as he opened the carriage doors. The dog hopped down reluctantly from Æsa's side and sauntered into the back. Not only was he safer back there, but he would act as a distraction should anyone look too closely into the carriage.

He glanced at her as they began to move toward the town, knowing all too well that hiccups could happen, but they had a few hours still. At least the sun was not present to dehydrate her even faster.

Banishing those thoughts as they neared the town, he gave Æsa one final encouraging statement: "I have an acquaintance who lives nearby, along the coast. He will replenish what we need, and he should be able to get a new tank for you. We can rest there for a few nights. Then—"

"The ocean." She closed her eyes and inhaled, her chest rose, and it looked like she developed some color just at the thought. Her skin was the pale that seemed to be upon all Sirens in the Kæ'vale area.

His story—should anyone ask—was that he was bringing his sickly cousin to a healer. Making their way through the town, they moved along with the traffic of horses, carriages, people on foot, and stray dogs dashing between the horse's legs. It was a busy place compared to the lonely road they'd been traveling, and that made Nikolai nervous. There was something about communities that always felt alive, reminding him that there was good in this world. While he did not crave such interaction, a deep part of him longed for some form of connection, something that could only be found if he interacted with others, which he struggled with.

The town was rife with action, and by the faces peering out of doorways and alleys, Nikolai knew something unsettled the townsfolk. Though he did enjoy the occasional visit to the towns and cities, he didn't usually have a Siren with him. This time coming through, the stakes were higher. Despite the cold, his hands began to sweat.

A small girl watched from the door of a shop selling cuts of meat, her eyes on Æsa with quiet curiosity. He wondered if she knew the little girl could tell Æsa wasn't human.

Up ahead, there was a roadblock—soldiers clad in Eiríkur's royal colors with the flags above them rippling in the wind. Nikolai gritted his teeth but showed no other concern than to alarm Æsa. As she soaked in everything about the town, having never seen so many people or inventions of Man before, Nikolai ensured the horses moved at a proper pace. Not too fast, not too slow. In the back of the carriage, there was only what a traveler might have. Clothes, food, some whiskey, and Kashmir. He'd even tossed Æsa's food to make sure that, should their carriage be checked, they would not find any sign of the Sea.

He just hoped they made it through quickly enough that she didn't start to feel the pain of being out of water. Continuing down the line of the checkpoint, each carriage took a few minutes of their precious time, and each individual who tried to talk their way out of it ended up getting a quick beating. It was taking ages, but Nikolai stayed still, only shifting when the line moved ahead. His horses clopped along the muddy ground a few steps at a time before coming to sudden halts each time the carriage ahead did. They reared their heads and snorted, their hot breath visible in the brisk air. Nikolai reached forward and stroked the rear of the most agitated horse, calming it slightly.

He noticed now the little girl moved alongside the carriage, sticking close to the storefronts. She was smiling at Æsa. Nikolai watched with frozen wonder as the girl came up to the carriage. Æsa looked down at the curious child and brought her gloved finger to her mouth, gesturing to keep quiet. The little girl grinned, nodded, and scurried back from the carriage. Realizing that the child saw Æsa for what she was but had no intention of telling the royal soldiers, Nikolai felt a swell of hope. The future would be shaped by the hands of girls like her.

"Next!" A soldier shouted, beckoning for them to come forward.

Nervously, Nikolai put on a calm face and continued ahead. He stopped when the soldier raised his hand, palm forward. Two soldiers walked around the carriage, and while one continued a full inspection, the other walked right up to Nikolai. Nikolai offered a pleasant smile.

"Anything that we should know about in the carriage, sir?" The soldier glanced beyond Nikolai at Æsa.

"Just myself and my sickly cousin." Nikolai took a deep breath, despair crossing his normally stern features. "We seek a healer," he paused to lean in and whisper to the man, "though I do not believe she will make the journey. What is it you folks are looking for?"

"None of your business, citizen."

"I understand." Nikolai nodded a few too many times, playing off as a dumb passerby. From his peripheral vision, he saw the other soldier had made his circle and was looking too closely at Æsa. Nikolai had to act fast; his heart beat loudly in his ears. Leaning over, he raised his blonde eyebrows at the soldier. "I would not get too close—she's pale as a ghost, about to become one, she is. I told her I would bring her to a healer to ease her sickly mind. Feel her head; she's as clammy as any dead girl would be."

The soldier reached up, and Nikolai's heart sank. Acting fast, Æsa recoiled, coughing violently. It was fake, but the soldier backed off and covered his mouth and nose. Nikolai was surprised she was so quick-witted, and he reminded himself to thank her for the save.

As if to top it all off, Kashmir stirred inside the carriage, and then soldiers perked up. "What do you have in the carriage, sir?"

"My fighting dog." Nikolai's tone turned almost to a growl; that dog was the one thing he cared about above all else in this world. "He does not take well to strangers, but he does listen to me. Go on, check, but do not get close."

They walked around the back and began unlatching the hitch. Kashmir started to bark wildly, causing a stir in the citizens all around. Nikolai's booming voice rang above all the noise, shouting for Kashmir to be silent. It was not only Kashmir that grew quiet; the whole street seemed to simmer down. Back behind the carriage, the doors were opened, and Kashmir paced, teeth bared for the show he had to put on. Quickly, the men shut the doors and latched it again.

The soldier came around, grimacing and visibly shaking. "Put that beast on a chain next time."

"He is locked in the carriage. I was not the one who opened it," Nikolai retorted. "He did not attack."

"He may."

"Are we free to go? My cousin might drop dead in this cold. We must be on our way."

"What healer were you going to see?" The soldier inquired suspiciously.

"Volmer." Nikolai threw a random name out. "He's well known. I'm sure you have heard of him."

The soldier put on a fake smile. "Ah, yes, very well known. Be on your way now and chain that mutt."

"Yes, sir." Nikolai agreed. He would never put Kashmir on a chain, but it was enough to say he would. The roadblock was finally behind them.

Nikolai kept the pace of the carriage smooth and comfortable until they were out of the soldier's sight. As soon as they were clear, he made the horses gallop as quickly as permitted with the carriage on the back. His nerves still had him reeling, and he never glanced at Æsa because he did not want her to see his fear.

19

ÆSA

Dawn was nearing, and Æsa knew that they were running out of time. Her throat was dry, and her insides felt like they were rotting. Like meat left out too long, she felt herself fester without water to keep her alive. Her hands clutched and balled inside the restricting gloves, the webbed area chafing. She refused to show Nikolai the pain she was in because he was already doing everything he could. A constricting feeling had wrapped itself around her throat nearly an hour prior, and it was closing in. Each breath felt like a thousand pinpricks.

Each minute that passed, each step the horses took rattled Æsa's bones. Trying to remain upright, she fought the urge to close her eyes and fade out. She had to remain alert at all costs: with the sun so close to rising, one mistake could cost either of them their lives. Her dry throat prevented her from crying out, unable to make any noise aside from a gentle wheeze of air. The horses moved faster at Nikolai's insistence, and that was when she could no longer hold herself up. Slumping over onto his broad shoulder, she gasped in pain.

"We're almost there," he said desperately, as if that would make the lake come closer. They could see the lake from the road.

The placid lake surrounded by low rolling hills was upon them at last. Small waterfalls trickled into the expansive body of water; it was far larger than the pond Æsa had been in before. In this lake, she could swim, stretch—*breathe.* The rocky land wrapping itself around the lake made the carriage bump and creak. They'd traveled nearly until the end of the night, both panicking, fighting the nature of time, defying it. She had never seen him so worried.

When they were near, the horses came to a light trot before stopping. Nikolai jumped off the carriage and rushed to the side where Æsa was, and she reached over and wrapped her arms around his neck as he carried her to the lake. Dropping to his knees in haste, he released her. Æsa leaped into the water, the scarf around her neck sliding from her, revealing her gills once again. They took in the oxygen from the water, and she was finally safe. She shed the clothing she bore and rose back to the surface.

Nikolai glanced once more at the horizon as if challenging the rising sun. He raised his hand with one finger up, signaling that he would be back in a minute. She swam freely, allowing her tail to splash water up into the bitter-cold air while she waited for his return. When he came around the carriage again, he held a spear in his hand.

"For protection," he explained as he handed it to her. "I hope you do not need it today, but I cannot leave you without something to ease my mind."

"Thank you, Nikolai..." She gripped the spear, recognizing the carvings in its handle. In her hand was a spear from the Great Wars, like the ones her Sisters used to take down Man. Árelía herself had a trident, and it was rumored to be the most beautiful artifact of the Sea. It was also in the clutches of The Mad King.

He nodded once before disappearing into the carriage for the day. Kashmir lay beside the horses, who never got a chance to be untied. The dog let out a mighty huff as if for relief that everything was calm and everyone was safe for the time being. Æsa sensed that, like some other animals, dogs could absorb the emotions of those around them and understand them better than humans could. It was obvious that Kashmir felt everything Nikolai felt, and the tired dog's eyes looked distressed. He shuffled over to the edge of the lake and lapped at the water, keeping a firm eye on Æsa.

The sun finally peaked over the surrounding hills, blinding Æsa for a moment as the white light consumed the landscape. She allowed her eyes the time to adjust, as it had been a while since she had seen the sun —traveling with Nikolai didn't allow for much daylight. She soaked in the gorgeous sunrise. The brilliant orb in the sky that gave everything in the world color saddened Æsa as she realized Nikolai had never seen the world like this. She hadn't either, not really. For most of her life, she lived so deep in the Sea that the sun was but a legend, like Árelía herself: she'd seen them both once or twice but could not remember much about either.

Though the lake was not like the home where she lived before all her Sisters perished, it reminded her of something that resembled a home. Perhaps it was the feeling of safety. Knowing she should rest but feeling unable to as she soaked in the beauty of the world around her, she thought back on her childhood. Though there wasn't much beauty in her memories, there were always parts that shined through the fire and darkness. Closing her tired eyes, Æsa let those memories inside of her finally come out. Before the fire, there was the Sea, and the Song that no longer had a tune. Peace and tranquility were all Sirens knew before Sól erupted.

Despite how badly Æsa wished to remember the faces of her fallen Sisters, all she could remember were their names and the ashes falling over the world, blanketing the sky in darkness. When Sól erupted, the world went black and gray. If her Sisters had not risen to the surface to help Man, they would all be alive today. Æsa wanted to scream at the skies and the Land, cursing them for destroying her peaceful species.

A cry of fear or agony escaped the carriage and tore Æsa away from her thoughts, bringing her attention to Nikolai. Hidden from the sun in the black carriage, curtains closed, Nikolai was attacked by his own memories and nightmares. Æsa saw him day after day, muttering in his sleep, fighting off his fears. Now, her anger turned to dread as she could do nothing to ease his struggles. When she glanced at Kashmir, the dog whined as if he, too, wished he could take away Nikolai's pain.

He would never find peace in this world.

They were both useless, but Æsa decided she would no longer be a burden to Nikolai. Gripping the spear, she tried to remember how her

Sisters used them, thrusting them at their attackers right into their hearts. Their fierce battle cries would ripple through the water as they attacked another ship, dragging Man to their watery deaths. Æsa would learn, she decided, for if she made it to the ocean again, she would need to defend herself. And Nikolai was the only one who could teach her.

20

NIKOLAI

Flat on his back in the carriage, hiding from the torturous sunlight that was only a curtain pull away from killing him, Nikolai found rest hard to come by. It was the first time Æsa had not been in the carriage with him during the day, and it did not sit right with him. Tossing and turning, he forced his eyes shut and draped the blanket over his head, but sleep evaded him mercilessly. He envied Man on days like this—they could walk the Earth day and night, and watch the sun rise and set. Nikolai had never seen the sun before, and, not for the first time, he truly craved it.

When Nikolai was finally granted sleep, it was filled with restless memories waiting just below the surface of consciousness. With decaying hands, they reached up, pulling him under as he found sleep, dragging him deep into the dirt in which they were buried. Motionless, except for the hammering of his heart in his chest, Nikolai was frozen as nightmares consumed him.

A thousand faceless ghosts from his past pulled him into true darkness. Only the sound of water dripping made his senses stir—everything else was numb. Unable to see, unable to smell, nothing touched him anymore. Nikolai could only hear the water dripping in the distance. Suddenly, a scream ripped through the air, shattering the serenity. Fear gripped Nikolai so tight that not even he could break its bonds.

"*Nikolai.*"

"Mother," Nikolai called back, desperate to find her. He could speak, he could breathe, but he did not feel his body.

"*Save me.*"

"I couldn't."

"*The last Siren is the key.*"

He had heard those words before, but where? When? It was not his mother who told him those words, so why was it her voice saying them now? Nikolai fought to move against the darkness, but when he did, he felt bony hands digging into him. No longer resisting, he reminded himself that this was a dream and that he just had to listen to what was being said. There was more importance in listening to what his own mind was telling him than there was in fighting against it. It was the key to unlocking what he needed to uncover.

"*Save me, Nikolai.*"

"I don't know how," he admitted. Was it Æsa he needed to save?

"*Balance within yourself.*"

Was it his mother?

Was it himself?

Nikolai woke with a start, his whole body covered in sweat. Shivering and too hot all at once, Nikolai yanked his shirt over his head and heard the fabric rip. Not caring, he used it to wipe the sweat from his head and neck, only then realizing how heavily he was panting. Outside the door, he could hear Kashmir whining and pawing at the wooden carriage. After a moment, he composed himself, then shifted out of the way of the window. When he drew the curtain, no sunlight came in. It was dusk at last.

Emerging from the carriage with haste as though the bad dream lingered there, Nikolai shuddered in the bitter cold air. With his shirt in the carriage behind him, Nikolai stripped off his trousers and boots. Circling around the carriage, he took one quick glance to ensure no one came near and that there had been no disturbance throughout the day. Kashmir crawled out from underneath the carriage and Nikolai instinctively reached down to pet the dog, then went straight for the water.

He did not see Æsa as he dove into the glacier-fed waters. It chilled him to the core, but he needed to wash the sweat from his body. Underwater for a few moments, he opened his eyes and saw nothing but complete blue. Inches away from his face, he would not have been able to see his hand. Surfacing, he took a deep inhale of the rich air and combed his fingers through his blonde hair. Hearing a splash, he turned and felt relief flood him when he saw Æsa's tail. She surfaced right in front of him, her shoulders and head above the rippling waters.

"Good evening," she said. She looked healthy for the first time since he laid eyes on her. Her back was healing nicely, and there was a smile on her lips. He was taken aback by how beautiful she was without pain lingering in her eyes. Even the burns on her face did not take away from her beauty.

Nikolai found himself speechless as if roles were reversed from when they first truly met.

She did not seem to mind or even notice his lack of response as she ran her webbed fingers along his arms. Her slender fingers revealed bones underneath, almost transparent in the webbing. They ceased at his tattoos—three rings around his right bicep in solid black. When she lifted his other arm, she fingered the delicate rings on the other bicep, which were broken up, incomplete circles. Her head cocked to the side as she studied them like a scholar, trying to discover their meaning without asking him.

"These are beautiful." She glanced up, hands still upon him.

He grimaced, feeling something heavy upon his shoulders as Æsa removed her hands. Sighing, he explained briefly, "The three rings are a symbol for being Pure Blooded. The other four are for each family member who was turned. My father, my mother, Roman, and Ivan."

"Do they too bear these symbols?" She looked like she wanted to ask about the others, the ones that painted his whole back and the faded lily on his hand.

"No." His reply was short. "We need to get a move on. Without the tank, we cannot afford to lose time."

They didn't speak as he brought her back to the carriage. When she crawled in, she felt the dampness of Nikolai's blanket and cast a glance in his direction.

"What haunts you?" she asked.

"Everything." He briefly closed his eyes, pinching the bridge of his nose. "Kash, in."

The dog leaped up, snuggling right up to Æsa as though she raised him. Her webbed hand went straight to the soft spot behind his ears that always made him kick his leg. Now he knew why Kashmir was so fond of being around Æsa, and the grimace on his face faded. "We will be there before morning."

Before he closed the carriage doors, she cocked her head to the side and said, "Nikolai?"

"Yes?" He glanced tentatively at her, worry etched on his features.

"Don't be so hard on yourself. We all have sins to atone for."

He studied her for a moment, curious, but dared not inquire. With a brief nod, he shut the carriage doors, submerging her in the darkness again. She inhaled the sweaty, stale air, wondering why he felt he had to suffer. She realized she was not ready to open up about what she had to atone for, and neither was he.

21

INTERLUDE

The silent, dusty castle where the Mad King Eiríkur lived his whole, pampered existence was brought back to life. Deep within the brick walls in the belly of the castle was where he had once worked to give his long-deceased wife legs. Many Sirens had been tortured here, and double that amount had been consumed in the dining room two floors above. Eiríkur felt a vigorous youth he had not felt since his last taste of Siren flesh six years ago. No longer the young man he was when he once rooted for and defended Sirens, his body had grown saggy in some areas and thin in others.

His bones were used to the ache and rattle, his lungs constricting painfully with each breath. Somehow, the mention of a Siren roused some of that youth within him, and walking no longer felt like a chore. He strode with vigor down the spiraling stairs, no pain in his previously rickety knees. Once again, his servants looked at him with respect. Their fear was still there, but where pity had lingered for years, respect flourished.

The only man who did not seem to fear him was Vlad, the strange Vampire with a keen interest in the man who held the Siren. At first, Eiríkur did not trust him, but he had proven himself efficient in his ways

—expending the armies to search carriages and houses, but not so many that costs became insurmountable.

To further prove that Vlad did not fear Eiríkur, he took command of nearly everything regarding the hunt for the Siren and Nikolai. Despite Eiríkur's demands, Vlad had deliberately disobeyed his orders to pursue the ringleader, Zidler. Though he had to admit, his reasons were indeed valid—the more people searching for her, the better. He had men on Zidler's scent: if he found the Siren first, the army would be close behind.

Not a day prior, Vlad had brought in a witness, someone he claimed had spoken with the Siren's capturer—A Witch posing as a barmaid. All they had gotten out of her over the last day and night was her name—Otávia. Eiríkur thought he recognized her and wondered if she was once a maid in his employ.

Down in the chambers, where years ago chemists and doctors had tested on and sliced open Sirens behind Árelía's back, a salty smell lingered. The scent of the Sea was trapped, haunting the dark walls. It was a wonder that their screams and pleas never kept him up at night. Shaking the thought from his head, he scanned the cruel devices used to get the Witch to speak.

He ran his fingers over ancient tools that had been boxed away many years ago, gripping his favorite. The cool steel against his hands made him shiver as though a ghost of the pain the tool once caused went through him. With his blue eyes glancing at the Witch, he crossed to where she was strapped down by leather bindings at her wrists and feet.

The denailing tool was small, appearing almost harmless, but it caused some of the worst pain. He pulled a chair up to where she was, their heads almost level. "Do you know what this is?"

She nodded, disgust on her face.

"I do not get enjoyment from hurting you," he lied. He glanced at the tool, holding it up in the candlelight, letting its presence linger so she could anticipate it.

"You are the Mad Prince. Of course you do," she spat at him, filled with fiery energy despite her suffering.

"King," he corrected sharply. Taking a calming breath, he looked Otávia in the eyes. "Tell me what you know about our Siren thief."

She did not move. She did not even flinch.

"You know where he is, where he is taking her, don't you?"

"I weep for help, for freedom," she pleaded innocence. "I am but a healer, a barmaid, a vagabond. Not a Witch. I fear my powers do not extend beyond healing common ailments."

"You call his name in your sleep. Nikolai. Vlad has confirmed he is the one with my prize," Eiríkur said, fingering the denailer.

She opened her mouth to speak but could not deny that she had learned his name through her craft.

Eiríkur grinned and slid his papery hand down her arm, trailing over tattoos and scars alike. When he reached her hand, he cradled it within his own. The small metal device was in his other hand, and he slowly waved it in front of her, showing her that he was capable of causing her pain if she did not speak. He did not know the extent of her powers, but if she could contact this Nikolai in her dreams, surely she could locate him. It would only take a bit of pain: every person had a limit.

It was time to find hers.

22

NIKOLAI

Three nights later, they arrived at a great white house. It stood tall atop the hill, overlooking a cliff that led down to the ocean. More a castle than a house, it was three stories tall with large windows that looked out over the lawns, all shut tight with blinds blocking onlookers and sunlight. Huge black doors contrasted with the pristine white paint, and upon them were heavy silver door knockers—fashioned as wolves holding rings in their sharp-toothed mouths. The symbolism was not lost on Nikolai.

He gripped one of the rings and knocked, booming noises that would echo through the entire house. The door opened, and Nikolai was greeted by a pale-skinned, blonde-haired beauty—Mihai Luca. The Vampire did not appear to have aged a day in the six years since Nikolai had seen him.

"Nikolai, Nikolai, Nikolai." His smooth accent bounced around the walls of the foyer. He held Nikolai's broad shoulders, kissing him on both cheeks. "To what do I owe the *pleasure*?"

Mihai spoke in a way that emphasized his words to sound more dramatic. He was all about flair—a seducer but a sneak, too. Nikolai couldn't help but smile at Mihai, thinking of the times they had spent together. "I need a favor."

97

Mihai gasped, holding a pale hand to his chest, pretending to clutch at his heart. "You mean this is not a visit for old times' sake? You only came to ask for my services? Nikolai, after everything I've done for you, I am disappointed."

"Have I ever come here as anything other than a friend needing a favor?" Nikolai countered.

"No." Mihai sighed, eyes turning to the brilliant sky. "And it does hurt me."

"You'll survive."

Mihai wiggled his shoulders, his way of agreeing. "So, what is it this time? Another Siren?"

"Yes." Nikolai learned almost everything he knew about Sirens from Mihai, including one important detail that sparked something in Nikolai ten years ago when he showed up at Mihai's doorstep in tattered clothing.

Mihai's smile curved up the corners of his mouth. He clapped and rubbed his hands together. He flashed a wicked grin, showing his teeth. "Do go on."

Nikolai made sure to skip over the fine details. Only trusting Mihai as far as he could throw him, he hoped to be here only long enough to obtain a new tank and give Æsa some time to recover. Then, they would be on their way again. If he did things right, there would be no other complications. For now, all he wanted was a warm bed to sleep in and a safe place for Æsa to swim in the true ocean. Her wounds would heal much faster that way.

The inside of the alabaster house was just as white as the exterior. It was a modern mansion with pristine walls that no one had ever laid a hand on. Art from around the world was scattered throughout, and strategically placed mirrors made the house feel like a museum.

Mihai never fit in with the rest of his family. His tastes were starkly different from his Luca ancestors. This was one of the reasons that Nikolai had to put his trust in the Luca—he had morals. His family had a Wolf-Man in their control, a Lycan who required a sacrifice and would wipe out entire bloodlines in a single night.

One of Mihai's distant relatives stood beside Nikolai's brother,

Roman. Nikolai always wondered if Roman's *Koroleva* could command the Wolf, but he hoped he did not need to worry about that. As the Wolf could only be commanded to slaughter an entire bloodline, Roman would never be able to use it against Nikolai without also being on the receiving end of the slaughter. He hoped the Witch did not have the ability to fine-tune that particular curse to meet Roman's needs.

It was agreed that he could stay for a while, and Mihai promised a tank for Æsa could be delivered in a few days. Only when Nikolai was granted assurance of his and Æsa's safety did he retrieve her from the hidden carriage in the woods. Kashmir trotted along, but Mihai would not let him in the house.

"You know my rules, Nikolai. No mutts in my house," Mihai said with a scowl.

The dog was to remain in the backyard. Nikolai frowned at Mihai's distaste for his best friend. He did not, however, blame him. Dogs and wolves were too similar for Mihai's tastes.

When he carried Æsa inside the mansion, she absorbed everything about the house. It was starkly different from his safe house. Having lived in the Sea meant that she hadn't seen much in her life, and Nikolai loved how she appreciated and noticed the little things. It was something he admired about her.

"You still have the indoor tank?" Nikolai asked Mihai.

"Only because I did hope for your return." Mihai gestured to the hallway, eyes on Æsa. "I presume you know the way."

Nikolai walked through the large house, down granite-floored hallways, passing all the dangerously placed windows. Æsa had her arms wrapped around Nikolai's neck, her head swiveling to look at everything. A particular statue made her stop, and when Nikolai glanced, he saw a stunning wood carving of a man transforming into a Wolf. Pressing his lips tight together, he avoided commenting. He was certain that since Æsa had not known about Vampires until recently, it was unlikely that she would know what a Lycan was. The statue was incredibly detailed—every ripple of muscle was distinct, and bones cracked through arms were torn open. To anyone who did not know the process of Lycan transformation, it would look like a horrible hybrid.

Nikolai hurried along toward the big room where he saw his first Siren. The tank was giant, the biggest tank Nikolai had ever seen. Though it was still too small to keep any living creature comfortably, it would do for now. He walked up the steps to the top of the cage, and Æsa's hands clutched his shirt. Her muscles tensed.

"Nikolai?

"Yes?"

"What about the ocean?"

He spoke in whispers in case anyone was eavesdropping. "Not until I've ensured the shore is safe. Mihai owns the land here. No one crosses onto his property, but I cannot trust Mihai as much as I would like. You cannot tell him anything. Do not tell anyone who comes to see you anything. Do not trust anyone here but me, do you understand?"

Nodding reluctantly, she sighed and took a deep breath, leaning her head on Nikolai's shoulder. Another day, another cage. But she was alive. Both of them looked at the large aquarium in wonder and disappointment. It was almost the height of the ceiling, with only a meter-tall gap at the top. It extended over the length of the wall, the only showpiece in the room. It was just another display like Zidler's show. Tall seaweed plants and large rocks within would allow Æsa to remain hidden, sit, or swim—she could do as she pleased.

Nikolai felt a wave of guilt when she hid immediately upon entering the tank. He pressed his hand to the glass, hoping she was listening. "I won't break my promise."

Heading back to the grand living room where Mihai waited, Nikolai flopped into a chair. The sitting room was a giant open space with a whole wall of windows overlooking the Sea. Nikolai and Mihai remained silent for only a few moments.

"She is quite the specimen. If I didn't know you better, I would have offered a pretty penny to keep her," Mihai started. He waved his hand over his face. "With a discount for the burns...although I would bet she has *quite* a story to tell."

"I do not agree with the buying and selling of any living thing," Nikolai countered.

"This is why I did not ask." Mihai gestured for Nikolai to sit on the leather couch beside him. He poured them both some whiskey, a subtle attempt to make Nikolai open up to him. He cocked his head to the side. "What troubles you, Nikolai?"

"You are familiar with Witches."

Mihai's smile faded into a grimace. "Unfortunately, I am very familiar. At least in the sense that, like most of my Luca relatives, I dislike Witches and the fact that Witchcraft runs through my veins."

"I had a few interactions with one, and I believe she is trying to communicate with me." Nikolai leaned back against the chair, realizing how comfortable it was after riding on a wooden carriage seat day after day. "Is this possible?"

"Possibly, yes." Mihai nodded. "Though no Witch can do such things. If what you are telling me is true, the woman you speak of must be a Seer. Do not answer, do not speak to her, do not even acknowledge her."

"It may be too late," he admitted. "I thought it was my mother in the dream."

"No surprise there. You are such a mother's boy." He laughed an airy chuckle. "Very unlike myself."

"Speaking of which, tell me this is not your family's doing. If I find out a certain Wolf is after me..." Nikolai's thoughts trailed back to Roman's Witch. He shuddered at the horrifying thought.

Mihai laughed, the sound seeming to boom through the house. "If that Wolf came after you, you'd be dead in an instant. No, Nikolai, you don't need to worry about my family coming for you. They care not for Vampires and Sirens. You know they cast me out when I became what I am now, as they do prefer their...dog."

"Do not compare Kashmir to that Curse." Nikolai scowled.

"My sincerest apologies."

"It's just..."

"My cousin is in bed with your brother?" Mihai raised an eyebrow. "Yes, well, if that curse could have been altered, it would have been done by now."

It was enough to ease Nikolai's mind.

Mihai finished off his whiskey in one gulp, then whistled a distinct note. Men and women entered through the doorways, most of them going straight to Mihai's side. He wrapped his arms around one man and one woman. "You are more than welcome to join us, Nikolai. Like old times."

Nikolai offered a smile. He rose from his seat and glanced around the room filled with beautiful people. "I am going to bed."

"Your loss," Mihai murmured as Nikolai disappeared down the hall, the sounds of giggles and moans filling the room.

23

ÆSA

When dusk fell a few evenings later, there was a cold wind blowing as Nikolai carried Æsa to the water. The ocean was black in the darkness, clouds covering the sky and moon. Little lanterns lit the switchback trail from Mihai's house to the water. Heart beating loudly in her chest, Æsa leaned forward as though trying to get out of Nikolai's grasp and into the Sea as quickly as possible.

"I know you're thinking of leaving," Nikolai told her. "I wish I could say it would be safe."

Æsa glanced at him, their faces close together as he strained to keep her steady.

"This cove is safe, but do you see those lights out there?" He thrust his chin out.

Æsa followed his gaze. Far out, where the inlet's rocky barrier ended and the ocean opened up to its vast expanse, lights dotted the water. Hundreds of boats waited with their nets in the water, hoping to capture a Siren. Waiting to capture *her*.

She nodded, unable to speak as despair crushed her. However, a small part of her felt relieved that she might stay in Nikolai's company a little longer. The Song of the Sea had been quiet for so long, but without other Sirens, there was nothing to return to.

Nikolai waded up to his knees when Æsa leaped from his arms and dove deep into the Sea. It wrapped its familiar arms around her, embracing her. Every part of her felt as though it was in its rightful place and had purpose again. The strong muscles within her tail moved as she navigated the waters, her webbed fingers spread wide for better speed and agility. After swimming for a while, she flipped onto her back below the surface, wishing she never had to go back up.

She could try to flee now. Perhaps she could evade the cluster of nets at the end of the inlet. Yet something tugged at her, telling her she could not leave Nikolai. There were answers she sought, and she knew he was the one who had them. The thought of swimming away without saying goodbye... It made her feel sick. Nikolai, over only a few weeks, had shown her there was good in this ugly world. When she surfaced, she wasn't sure if she wanted to go on living in a world so empty. The Sea would always be empty, and it pained her to know that she wanted companionship. She did not want to part with Nikolai.

Not yet.

She had a feeling there were things he wasn't telling her, and hope bloomed within her chest at the thought that there might be more to where he planned to take her. Something told her she needed to go with him to the end of this journey, even if she was one decision away from freedom and safety now.

Darkness surrounded her. She could not tell the bottom from the top just by looking, but her instincts told her which way was up. Her near-white hair swirled all around her, obscuring her vision. When she surfaced, at last, Nikolai sat on the rocky beach with a fire going beside him. Æsa was impartial to the cold—she never knew anything else. Nikolai, however, preferred a bit of warmth. Sitting on the beach on a cold night was hard on anyone. Æsa came right to the shore, propping herself up on her side with her tail in the water. Glancing at him, she finally decided that it was time to ask him to teach her how to defend herself like her sisters could.

"Where did you learn to fight?" Æsa asked him.

He looked surprised by her question but smiled at the memory. "When you grow up with brothers like mine, you learn to fight at a young age. When I was a teenager, we would bet on back alley fights, and then, one day, I joined in. Turns out I was pretty good at it.

"The fighting pits were some of the only places I ever felt like I fit in. The men that I fought didn't know what I was. They were all there for the same reason as me—to prove a point, to have a little fun, to win some coin." Nikolai leaned forward, resting his forearms on his knees and picking at some driftwood on the ground. He tossed bits of wood and dried seaweed into the fire, watching it crackle.

"You harbor so much guilt," Æsa noted.

He glanced up. "The fights taught me something, Æsa. They taught me perspective. I was on the same level as Man, as Siren, as Vampire, as Werewolf. And yet, I stood at the front of the Brotherhood, acting like I was equal to them while being treated far better than they were. The hypocrisy disgusted me."

He picked at a scab, eyes downcast.

"I killed so many brothers in the name of equality."

Æsa knew what she had to say. It would not make Nikolai feel less guilty, but perhaps it would give him even more perspective. More insight into her own past might help him understand that no one was truly good or bad. Everyone has something that keeps them up at night, memories that taunted and swirled through their mind, haunting them. Maybe hers did not torment her as much as Nikolai's, but what haunted her happened when she was so young that it was only a faint memory now.

"I was very young when Árelía married Eiríkur, and it seemed as though everything was going to be okay for us. For Sirens. I was so young and naïve. When the Wars began, I was still a child. I watched my Sisters leave for battle, and now I understand that the look in their eyes was not determination but the knowledge that they would not come back.

"You see before Sól erupted, the last male Siren died. We do not know why. I was the youngest, and so, I suppose, they wanted to protect me. I was taken to a safe place where I was raised, trying to ignore the Great Wars going on all around me. But each day, more and more of my Sisters disappeared. I wanted to help them, so I went to the surface to fight. Those who swore to protect me came for me, and so many died that day. Right before my eyes. The Sea turned black with their blood... I fled when I realized what I had done."

"So, you went back to the depths of the Sea." Nikolai's words were soft, as though he were speaking to the dead Sirens and not Æsa. Rising to his feet, he waded right into the water, and when she didn't follow, he said, "Come on then."

"For what?"

"You want to learn how to fight."

"How did you...?"

"I've seen that look before, Æsa."

She crawled back into the water, waves lapping at her skin. The night sky was like pitch now, so dark that one who was not accustomed to such would be unable to see their hand in front of their face. But they were used to it. She swam right up to him. He peeled off his shirt and tossed it to the shore, standing waist-deep in the water.

"Take me down," he commanded. "Try to drown me."

Æsa was foolish in her first attempt as she charged him head-on. Nikolai gripped her arms as she neared, shoving her aside. She bent her tail so that it forcefully pushed against the movement, and it slowed her down and gave her rigidity. With his hands gripping her wrists, she couldn't use them. He released them and backed up.

"Again."

She threw herself backward, diving deep into the water. Hidden from his view but still able to sense him, she realized she had the advantage. Pondering the best route to go against a seasoned fighter, she decided that the legs would be a good start. She swam slowly at first to avoid disturbing the waters above her, the waves giving her some leeway, then she gripped his ankles with both hands. Pulling back, she found that she was unable to make him budge. Nikolai had his feet planted so firmly that Æsa could not move him. She surfaced, looking to him for guidance.

"Use the water to your advantage. Do not come up on me slowly; you need force behind your actions. A running punch will have more force than a standing one," he explained. "Again."

Æsa lingered under the water this time for a while, hoping to throw Nikolai off from her position. She had come at him both times now from the deep end, but this time, she circled around him to come at him from the shoreside. He was facing the ocean, not the land, expecting her to come from that direction again. Though she had less cover, she now had the element of surprise. The water was just deep enough for her to get up to a quick speed, and she charged at his hips, slamming her shoulder into his waist. Knocking him off his feet, Æsa gripped tight as she used her tail to force him under the water. When he was deep enough, she released him so he could go up for air.

They both surfaced, and Nikolai shook his head, gasping for breath. He slicked his blonde hair back with a grin. "That was good, you're learning fast."

"I have a good teacher."

Still grinning, he said, "Again."

24

NIKOLAI

Nikolai was soaking wet and lying on the shore. The waves lapped at his toes, a gentle kiss before it pulled back. The tide was going out, though it didn't move much on this small spot of shore that Mihai owned. If there was one thing about Kæ'vale that Nikolai would miss should he never see it again, it was the night sky over the ocean. Though it was seasonal, there was nothing quite like watching the Aurora light up the night sky.

Æsa lay beside him, half in the water, with her hands behind her head and her bright white hair sprawled around her. She turned to face him. He could feel her studying him, assessing him with that observational gaze. "What if you went back?"

"To Osleka?" Nikolai met her gaze.

"To the Brotherhood."

Shuffling, Nikolai realized that he had wondered that many times in his life. He was growing older, and one day, he would have to face his problems. He had been running for a decade and had taken back as much control of his own life as a broken person could. Nikolai spent a lot of nights looking over his shoulder, expecting to see his brother smiling wickedly with that dead look in his eyes. Should Roman show up right then and there, Nikolai would face him as he knew he would have to one day.

His tongue reached back into his mouth and felt where his molar was missing. A gaping hole where his tooth used to be, just like the gaping hole that had been ripped in his heart when he found his mother dead. When he tried to fight Roman, his brother defeated him. But Roman had made one mistake—he took the advice of a woman who showed mercy. That day, Roman lost his hold on him. Ten years later, he was still searching.

Nikolai knew it was the only time Roman showed mercy, and he regretted it. He would not offer it the next time he found him. And Nikolai could not run forever.

"He would probably kill me," Nikolai said. Once the words were out, they sounded all too probable.

"You are safe here, yes?" She rolled onto her side with her arm outstretched, resting her head on her bicep.

It was in the way that she looked at him, with so much trust, that he was strong and able to protect her that made him lie. He had no doubt Roman was coming for him, and he was terrified of what might happen when he caught up. As long as Æsa was safe, he would accept his fate. He suspected that Æsa would be the last one.

"Yes, I'm safe here," Nikolai said. There was the essence of hope that it could possibly be true. He could handle one or two of the things haunting him, but if all of them came for him at once, he knew he would fail.

A woman came down the switchback trail, wearing a white dress with a slit that caused the fabric to reveal her legs with each step. With a bewitching stare from cold, mismatched eyes, she glared down at the two soaking wet, half-nude people on the beach.

"Mihai wishes for you to join him for supper," she told Nikolai coldly.

Nikolai leaned his head back, looking at her upside down. "Does he realize we are Vampires, and it is terribly awkward to eat together?"

She raised her lip, then crossed her arms like a frustrated mother. "Do I have to repeat myself?"

"Please don't," Nikolai snorted.

Æsa giggled beside him, then rolled onto her stomach to get a better look at the woman. "Am I invited?"

Instead of replying, she turned and began the ascent to the house.

With a groan, Nikolai rose. His body was tired from all his work with Æsa, but she showed much improvement in the few hours they had been out there. He would have to bring the spear next time. Grabbing his semi-damp shirt, Nikolai slipped it over his head and then rose to his feet. Lifting Æsa was not difficult on most occasions, but she felt much heavier after a full night of training. Still, he prevailed, making it to the top of the cliff and to the house in a matter of minutes.

Back in the house with Æsa in the tank, he leaned against the glass. "Remember, trust no one. We will practice more again tomorrow night. It won't be long before we leave here. We are very close now."

"To what?" Æsa asked with desperation in her eyes, arms propped up at the top of the tank so she could speak to him.

Nikolai was too afraid to give her hope in case it was ripped away. "You'll see," he replied, then quickly left.

Though Vampires had very little use for dining rooms, Mihai kept the traditional make-up of a house when he had it built. Perhaps it was to fool guests that he would coax over during the night to devour. Nikolai never asked. As he snaked his way through the winding hallways, he heard screaming coming from the dining room. Never one to feed on innocent people, Nikolai grimaced at the thought of who he might be offered to eat tonight. Turning down a gift or gesture from a Luca was a risky decision, though. The Lucas were an unpredictable family at best.

Nikolai stepped into the large dining room decorated with large sculptures of nude men and women, all surrounding a table made from one slab of wood from a giant red oak tree. Chairs with carved filigree and velvet cushions were spaced around the table, and in two of these sat a man and a woman with terror etched onto their faces.

"Nikolai!" Mihai clapped his hands together. "I know your...dietary choices differ from my own, so I have catered to your *ethics* tonight."

"Mmm?" Nikolai didn't take his eyes off the two strapped down. The woman had long, mousy brown hair that was thin as paper. Beside her was a man who was certainly older than her, his bald head also glistening with sweat. His bushy eyebrows were furrowed in anger.

"These two were well known back in the day as Siren traders," Mihai walked around the head of the table and stood between the couple, an arm on either of their shoulders. His head between theirs, he glanced at them. "Weren't you?"

"No!" the man exclaimed. "No, we never traded any—we never did!"

"No?" Mihai pouted. At the head of the table where he had been standing was a box. Pulling out dried flesh that was unmistakably Siren, he dangled it in front of them, "You thought it was fish then? Paid thousands for some dried fish? I do not think so."

"Please," the woman spoke softly through gentle sobs. "I did not know. It was my husband's doing. Our daughter—"

"Dalla!" The man shouted at her.

"Nikolai, need you more proof? I'm positively famished." Mihai cast a glance that an unsuspecting person might believe to be innocent.

Nikolai nodded, hating the show Mihai had to put on just for dinner. Agreeing to his terms and silently appreciating that he went out of his way to find people who had done harm, Nikolai decided to feed on the woman, Dalla. Mihai was a cruel man when he wanted to be; he played with his food. Though they might have done horrible things in the past, Nikolai didn't think they were deserving of pain. He walked over to the woman and turned her chair to face him.

"I am sorry," he whispered and then used the flat of his hand to push her head back, thus exposing her neck. Fangs penetrated her flesh, and he could taste the salty sweat that clung to her. Once the iron-flavored blood hit his taste buds, Nikolai shut his eyes and shuddered, not wasting a drop as he quickly had his fill. Only when he finished did he realize that the man, her husband, was screaming.

Nikolai glanced over, wiping blood from his lips. Mihai had sliced a small hole in the man's throat and put a small spile there. Handcrafted for Vampires who liked to torment, the spile allowed for blood to flow when they wanted it, and they could shut off the valve to save it for later. Mihai used a crystal glass to collect the blood, as he claimed it was more savory to do so. Having come from a low-class family, Mihai spared no expense to show off his wealth now. He left behind his status but kept the Luca cruelty.

The man was sobbing, tears dampening his dirt-covered shirt.

"I am sorry," Nikolai repeated, quickly leaving the room.

25

ÆSA

When Nikolai had left Æsa in her tank, she tried not to let it darken her spirits. Loneliness had been so ingrained in her life that she feared it now. Each time she was apart from Nikolai and Kashmir, her heart rate rose, a nervous tick filling the void they left behind. The tank worsened such feelings, but she reminded herself over and over that she was on the way to safety.

Which made her wonder if she would ever see Nikolai again after he got her there. *If* he got her there. Thinking back on when she had asked if he had done this before—brought a Siren to safety—his answer was clear, but she still had questions. While he seemed confident that he could get her there, she wondered how many times he had succeeded in the past. Her ponderings swirled in the water with her, alone in the tank, where she could not avoid the crushing feeling of loneliness and fear.

With the fear came the torrent of guilt.

The eldest Siren, and first in command now that Árelía was dead, had told her what she needed to do to survive.

"Æsa, my Sister, you must stay hidden." Eyvör had gripped Æsa's shoulders as the Great War above raged on.

Beams sunk down through the waters, charred from the fires. Eyvör looked at the catastrophe around them before her eyes landed back on young Æsa. She was but a child, naught more than seventeen winters—too young to be thrown into battle. That's what they told her, but it was her status as the youngest and last Siren they chose to fight to protect her at all costs. Eyvör, the eldest, and Æsa, the youngest—so different, and yet they wanted the same outcome—to live out their lives with only the memory of Man.

Man was evil.

"I just want to fight," Æsa begged, looking around at the horrors that found her in the depths of the Sea. Dead ships harboring Man killed by Siren's hand. All she wanted was to contribute to the cause, to give her life if she had to.

She didn't understand that they were fighting for her, the last of their kind.

"Æsa, you are a child!"

"I grew up with war—I know nothing else! I will not have another Sister die for me."

Eyvör clutched her tighter, but before she could speak, Æsa broke from her hold and yanked the spear from her clutches. Determined, she swam as fast as she could to the raging battle above her. Dozens of ships covered the surface, blocking out the light from the sun. With the fires burning, it was impossible to tell if it was night or day from below. She could hear her Sisters shouting for her to stop, many of them giving up their own battles to protect her. She was so naïve.

And it had gotten her Sisters killed.

She was shaking when she was torn from her reverie. For ten years, it was all she thought of, day after day, with nothing to distract her. It was a wonder that she had not lost her mind, though she imagined Nikolai might call it strength. She looked down at her hands, one slightly burned, and knew she was weak. Until she did something for someone else instead of for herself, she would not be strong.

Her foolishness cost her the chance to do that ten years ago, but now she had the opportunity.

"Good evening." The same young woman who had called Nikolai to dinner appeared. She had the essence of a flower about her as she pressed her hand to the glass. She bore a white dress; the fabric cinched tight at her waist to show her petite frame.

Nikolai told Æsa not to trust anyone, so she stared at the young woman. She could be no older than twenty, if that. With yellow-blonde hair and large mismatched eyes, she looked so welcoming and kind and as naïve as she had once been.

"My name is Fía," she told her. "You are Æsa?"

It was far too easy for her to resort back to being mute.

But Fia did not leave. "My mother told me Sirens were the guardians of the Sea. Is that true?"

Æsa swam to the top of the tank, above water.

"Maybe once we were."

"You fought so hard for your safety. I envy you."

"I did not fight," Æsa admitted bitterly, the taste of self-loathing on her tongue. "I cowered for years."

"As would I." Fía wrinkled her nose, the freckles that dotted her round cheeks making her look so much younger. "I am a coward... That is why..." she trailed off.

Æsa felt uncomfortable in her presence, her innocence washing away, the doe-look in her eyes turning vicious. Refusing to show fear, Æsa stared her down. From the arched doorway came another person, a dark-skinned man with piercing eyes. He wore simple trousers and no shirt. Various tattoos crossed the skin over his chest and around his back. He stood beside the young woman, never taking his eyes off Æsa.

"Isn't she beautiful, Davi?" Fía asked him, her soft tone sour.

"Nature's finest creation." Davi cocked his head to the side, admiring Æsa. "She deserves to be seen throughout the world. We deserve to see her kind."

"I could not agree more," another voice said from the arch. With orange hair like fire, Zidler walked in using a cane to keep himself steady, ugly black burn marks on his face. He reached the tank where Æsa had recoiled at the sight of him and placed a gloved hand on the glass, looking up at her. "We are not so different now, Siren."

Æsa began to shake her head. Where was Nikolai? Where was Kashmir?

"I've come to take you home, Æsa."

"What have you done with him?" Æsa asked.

"Oh." Zidler smirked. "He is being well taken care of. Do not worry."

26

NIKOLAI

Staggering away from the dining room, Nikolai began to feel fuzzy, as though he was drunk. Senses spinning, he quickly realized something was terribly wrong. His hands clutched at the air, then pressed hard against the walls. Fighting to remain standing, Nikolai fell against a statue of a woman standing tall and strong in the hall. The arm was perfectly extended as though offering to help him, but the face of the woman was not helpful or sincere.

The tightness in his throat spread. A grunt managed to escape as his grip on the statue faltered. There were only two reasons for him to fight this feeling—Kashmir and Æsa. As he began to crawl, he heard soft footsteps coming from behind him. With all his determination and might, Nikolai could not even grab the curved dagger he carried in his coat pocket to protect himself. The potency of the drug was too much, even for him.

A woman stood beside him, and he noticed an anklet bearing a fin resting daintily above her foot.

Nikolai asked, "Were y-your parents purists?"

She used her foot to push Nikolai's shoulder back, letting him look up at her. She looked so young, like a teenager, but Nikolai knew she was older than that. He realized it was the same woman who called him in for dinner.

"You ate my mother." She crouched down and placed his soft hand upon his stubble-covered cheek. "My name is Fía. My mother was Dalla, and my father Jón. He is still alive, but barely."

"W-why?" Had Nikolai known one of Mihai's guests was the daughter of his dinner, he would have gone out and found something—someone—more suitable. He did not understand why Mihai had done this.

"Oh," Fía explained. "You see, they raised me on Siren flesh, and I have a taste for it more than Eiríkur ever did. Now I made a deal—"

"I'll kill him." Nikolai tried to pull himself along, but his arms were now too weak. Someone else entered the hallway.

"When she dies of natural causes, Davi and I will get her body to feast upon." A smile filled her voice.

The man, Nikolai presumed this was Davi, extended his hand, and Fía took it, rising to stand.

"Grab him."

Davi reached down and hooked his arms underneath Nikolai's and began to drag him along the cold floor. The only thing that Nikolai could think of was how slowly he would kill Mihai if he ever got the chance. While he knew he could not do anything to prevent this, he could do one thing for sure: to increase his chances of getting all three of them out of this alive and in one piece.

He listened.

Kashmir was not barking—an odd thing, but not entirely unusual since he was outdoors and was missing out on the chaos. He could hear voices, many of which he did not recognize. Trying to piece together why Mihai would have betrayed him was harder. He had all the money, men, and women that he wanted in life: what they could have offered him to give them Æsa's corpse was beyond Nikolai.

He decided that it was their lives: Fía and Davi had offered themselves for Mihai to own forever—he did have a taste for couples. He loved to watch—he loved to get involved between the sheets. They were a comely couple, but it still did not seem enough. Their servitude and silence for Mihai owning Æsa until her death…seemed low, even for a Luca.

Nikolai lost his sight—but not his hearing—by the time he stopped moving. Tuning into his other senses, he listened with intrigue and desperation. Clanging metal echoed in an empty room. Ropes appeared, binding his wrists. He tried to fight, tried to summon the strength to move so that he could stop this. He received a hard kick to the stomach and toppled over.

As an avid fighter, Nikolai was not used to being defenseless. His heart hammered in his chest. He felt someone tying him up. Their hands were soft, like those of someone who lived in privilege, with a roof always over their head. Some people knew luxury their whole lives, and they did not care who they had to kill to get what they wanted.

Nikolai was tied up, bound to, and leaned against a wall. He slurred his words. "Tell Mihai h-he wi-ill pay."

A sharp laugh like ice water. Fía. "Oh, I will tell him, Nikolai."

Then silence.

The moment that Nikolai was alone, the severe anxiety that came with failure overcame him. He failed a Siren only once before, and it haunted him. She would slip into his dreams at night, turning them from serene to sinister. Sif—that was her name. She had a strength that made her beautiful. She fought so hard for her chance at life, but Nikolai had failed then, and he feared that he was failing again. But Æsa was different; Nikolai could not bear to fail her. He regretted not telling her to flee when she was in the ocean earlier that night—perhaps she would have evaded the hunters. It was selfish of him to think she couldn't have made it. It was selfish of him to want her to stay with him a while longer.

And yet, he knew she stayed because he promised her a safer place with other Sirens. He never told her he was taking her to more of her kind because he couldn't bear to disappoint her, but he knew she suspected as much. Now, it didn't matter. He would die, and Æsa would suffer until she perished. His thoughts began to devour him from the inside.

All he could do was think about his shortcomings and wait. The silence sank in, weighing down on him like a thousand bricks, crushing his bones like he was a Witch on trial. The Witch—no, the Seer, Otávia. He wondered if she was on his side. Could he save her? Nikolai knew that he couldn't risk his life for every innocent that needed his help, but it still ate away at him when he lost someone. Even someone he did not even know.

His mother. His best friend. His lover. Sif.

He failed two people today.

Æsa.

Kashmir.

27

ÆSA

Æsa sank to the bottom of the tank, her webbed fingers pushing her away from the glass. The tank was deep, and if anyone tried to come in to get her, she could drown them. She would use her sharp nails to slash at them until they bled to death. She would bite into their flesh with her teeth like Nikolai did. She would do anything to stop them from taking her.

Two familiar faces appeared: Ansel and Brutus. Both of them were in worse shape than she last saw them, and she felt pride for Kashmir. Her thoughts momentarily went to the dog, hoping that he was okay. She saw what he meant to Nikolai. Before she could do anything, Brutus lifted a metal bar. Approaching the tank, he leveled the bar with the center of the glass.

She heard Zidler say, "Do it."

Brutus swung the bar and slammed it against the glass. Æsa cried out in pain, the vibrations ripping through her. He did it again and again until the glass cracked. She looked for a way to escape, but she could not pull herself out of the tank and drop to the ground. They would catch her. Instead, she prepared herself for what would inevitably happen when the glass broke. Another crack began to leak, and she could feel the rush of the water being pushed out of the tank.

One more heavy slam and a great hole appeared. Water gushed free, but Brutus didn't stop. Æsa felt herself being pulled toward the opening, her hands grasping to hold onto anything at all. But when the whole wall shattered, glass blending with the waterfall that burst onto the floor, she went with it. It sucked her toward the waiting men, the glass shards shredding her arms and tail. All she could do was cover her face and try to protect herself.

When she hit the ground, Æsa pushed herself up to attack anyone who came near, but Brutus slammed the metal bar against the side of her head, knocking her out cold.

ORANGE AND YELLOW SURROUNDED ÆSA. She would never have believed that she could hate color after being deprived of it for so many years, but she hated orange and yellow. Fire was orange and yellow, and Zidler's circus was the same. Æsa hated the sight of those striped tents surrounding her. She hated being trapped inside another glass tank— the same one as before. This time, there was less water so that she could rise above it. Now that Zidler knew she could speak, he would demand more from her. She would not give it.

Strong scents of smoke came from every direction. There was laughter and cheering in celebration of getting her back. Æsa touched the bruising spot just below her eye; she had tried to fight, but a Siren out of water was out of her league.

She was alive for now, but was Nikolai?

To her surprise and joy, Zidler had not come in since she'd been plopped into that tank, which had not been cleaned and was slightly blackened from the fire Nikolai had set. He was out enjoying the celebration, and Æsa was left to think about Nikolai and Kashmir. Aside from her dead Sisters, they were the only two beings in the world that Æsa cared for anymore. She'd seen so much evil in Man, and never once had she seen gratitude or kindness. She had only found that in the form of a Vampire and a dog. The world of Man was filled with lies and deceit, and she wanted no part of it.

The tent flap parted quite a while later. She knew that they traveled throughout the daylight but had made camp before the sun fell. Longing for answers, Æsa was thankful when she noticed Fía enter the tent.

"What did you do with Nikolai?" she asked Fía as she rose up.

"I imagine he is quite dead by now, hours ago when the sun rose." She feigned sincerity. "I heard that burning to death as a Vampire is quite horrible. It's a shame he had to go that way, but we didn't want him to be identifiable post-mortem."

Æsa's heart sank, and she sank with it. The heaviness of Nikolai's death weighed on her shoulders; just one more death to add to her endless list. Every part of her shook as she dug her nails into the palms of her hands, black blood beginning to swirl in the dirty water. She refused to cry in front of this evil woman who looked so innocent and kind.

"Did you know that Mihai had rooms specifically to kill his own kind with the sun?"

Æsa refused to speak, finding herself incapable of muttering anything in her overbearing sorrow.

"He was a very disturbed man." Fía grinned. "But I suppose all Night-walkers are. Even your Nikolai, whom you clearly thought so highly of. He killed my mother, although that was partially at my own hand. The sacrifice had to be made, as they couldn't keep up with my demands. This was the only way I could get my hands on another Siren. Though, unfortunately, I have to wait until you're a corpse."

The tent parted once again, and Zidler entered with Brutus and Ansel. Kashmir had done a lot of damage to them, and Æsa had to conceal her pleasure at again seeing Brutus's maimed face and Ansel's missing fingers. Even if they were gone now, she would look at burned Zidler and deformed Brutus and Ansel, knowing full well which had caused them such agony.

"I see our little devotee has made herself known to you, Æsa." Zidler glanced at Fía with distaste.

Should Fía want to eat Æsa sooner, she could kill her. Should Zidler want that threat and worry out of the way, he would kill Fía. It would not take long for one or the other to break their end of the deal, leaving it to crumble in on itself. Æsa only hoped that it would be Zidler. At least then, she might live a few more years.

"She has likely also informed you that your Vampire friend, er..."

"Nikolai," Æsa growled.

"Yes, Nikolai has since met his end. It is a shame: I would have loved to have a former Brotherhood leader in my show. All that muscle, he could have done so much. Perhaps turn all the beautiful ladies into Nightwalkers... For a fee, of course." He frowned when Æsa refused to give him a reaction. "We started off on the wrong foot, I understand. I am willing to give you another chance to live a pampered and rich life, should you accept. I want to give you everything you could ever hope for: you need only speak the command, and it will be met."

"Bring back my Sisters," she snarled. "Bring back Nikolai and Kashmir."

"The mutt?" He frowned. "I suppose I could get you the mutt, but Brutus and Ansel might eat him for dinner. Better him than you, yes?"

There was a chance that Kashmir was still alive, and somehow that made Æsa feel better. The sinking feeling of inevitable sorrow seemed a little less horrible to face, knowing the most innocent of creatures might still be alive. However, Æsa knew that without Nikolai, it would not be a life worth living. That dog lived and breathed for him—without him, he would only suffer.

"Fía, get out." Zidler waved his hand, and the woman left with a scowl. Zidler didn't even glance at her, keeping his eyes on Æsa the whole time. "I think you at least owe me some gratitude. I saved your life. I am giving you a home where I can protect you. The others who live here are always thankful for the safety I grant them. Safety from the cruelness of society."

"Nikolai snuck me out from right under your nose. What makes you think Eiríkur can't do the same?" Æsa knew the dangers that followed her just for being what she was.

A creature of the Sea.

"Last time, I made mistakes—ones I will not make this time. We are beginning the journey off of Kæ'vale tomorrow. Only one last show until we are on the mainland," Zidler explained, then shifted on his good leg, leaning on his cane.

"We are not so different, you and I," he said, tapping the burned marks on his face. "Please try to keep an open mind, Siren."

He left the tent, and one more person came in to visit her.

Deformed, disgusting to look at—that's how Æsa would have described the beast that hobbled in. His face was covered with thick hair on one half, and his shoulders and back were horridly hunched, the bones protruding and almost splitting the flesh with his every movement. Bright green eyes bore into her as he stared at her. His claws were too long for his human hands, and his feet were too large for shoes. He looked like the statue Mihai had in his house, except that statue was a muscular man combined with some sort of creature. This thing before her was hideous.

"I've come to exp-p-plain," he said softly, his voice sounding like gravel. "I understand that you are in a diffi-c-c-cult place. But you w-will find a home here. I am ac-c-cepted here and n-n-no place else."

Æsa stared coldly at the Half-Man, Half-Wolf creature in front of her. The game he was playing, whether he knew he was even playing it, was not one she would fall for. Zidler expected her to see this creature being accepted as a good thing he had done. Perhaps for him, but she had been ripped away from any good in her life time and time again. It was time to admit exactly how she felt about it.

The Man-Wolf continued to speak of the kindness that Zidler had extended to him when Æsa cut him off.

"My home was with Nikolai," she said, then shut her mouth, intending not to open it ever again.

28

NIKOLAI

Nikolai woke to screams. Startling cries from nearby echoed through the pristine walls of the house, rousing him. When his weary pupils focused at last, he saw that he was in a small room, naked and bound to the wall by a rope. Shaking his arms, he heard the clang of a metal hoop against the wall. Only when he realized what sort of chamber he was in did it register in his mind exactly how disturbed Mihai was.

Though they may not have had much trust between them, Nikolai would once have considered him a friend. He came to Kæ'vale ten years ago with nothing but fear in his heart and rags on his back, and Mihai took him in. Mihai, who had no connection to the scraggly, sad excuse of a person who showed up at his door, offered him companionship and protection. Mihai was the person to set Nikolai down the path of helping Sirens, even though he preferred to display them in his home. In the six years since he last saw Mihai, he had changed. Though Nikolai never trusted him fully, he had trusted him enough to take this risk.

And now it was going to cost him his life.

And Æsa's.

Anger burst through him as he tried to pull the rope from the wall, but it refused to budge. The screaming in the other room did not stop.

He had to get free, or he was next. Noticing that the door itself was cracked open, Nikolai thought sourly that it was just another way to taunt him. To show him just how close he was to freedom.

Nikolai looked up at the open window and wondered how much time he had before the sun made its way to his room. Whoever was in the room next to his made sounds only a dying Vampire would make—desperate cries for the pain to stop. Man had many ways of serving the death sentence: hangings, burnings on pyres, crushed by rocks.

Vampire executions were almost always done by the sun.

Maybe he deserved this death, but Nikolai was not ready for it just yet. There were still too many lives at stake, lives he had sworn to protect. After he reminded himself of this, he was calm once again. The window was bright, but the sun had not yet come far enough to breach it. He had a few minutes, at best, before it began creeping in. Feeling the ropes with tired fingers, he tried to decipher the knot, but his mind was still foggy from the drugs that lingered in his system.

Hands sweating as he fumbled with the ropes, Nikolai made no headway. When the screaming stopped, he paused for a moment to wonder who else had been betrayed by Mihai. He had not known there was another Nightwalker in their midst. The corner of the window lit up bright with sunlight; the light shone on the ground beside Nikolai's foot. He pulled his legs closer to his body and knelt like he was truly about to be executed. The movement allowed him to turn his head around and look at his bonds.

The knot was unfamiliar to him, with no end nor beginning to untie it. Inch by inch, the sun crept closer, crawling toward him like a spider, fangs bared. His heart pounded, sweat beading upon his forehead. Droplets fell as though he simply basked in the sun, but he wouldn't sweat when it touched him; he would char like someone had placed his flesh directly onto an open flame.

The sun reached his knees and began to burn him. A scream ripped from his throat as the sun began to consume him—the pain was like nothing he had felt before. Not even losing his mother hurt this much.

He nearly fell over in pain. The door nudged open just a crack, revealing the familiar black snout of his best friend. The metal door screeched open, and Kashmir pounded into the room. He went straight for the ropes, pulling hard to save the life that mattered most to him. His sharp teeth sliced through the ropes, and Nikolai leaned away from the sun as it came closer and closer. Once the ropes were gnawed at enough, Nikolai tugged, and the bonds broke. He crawled out of the room.

He panted heavily as he lay on his back in the hallway, safe from the sunlight. He covered his face with his hands and released a throaty scream.

Kashmir whined, nuzzling Nikolai with a damp nose.

"Why, Kash?" His voice broke.

The dog barked.

Nikolai sat up, thankful that Kashmir was alive and well. He pulled the dog close and hugged him, kissing the dog on his soft forehead. He was shaking when he said, "You are my sweetest friend, Kashmir."

Using the wall to steady himself, he looked at the burns on his knees. They were bright red, and he knew he would heal soon. Only when Vampires began to char was there concern: there was no coming back from that. A blackened burn meant perpetual agony, and he had known many Nightwalkers who chopped off the limb to avoid suffering.

He found his clothes in a pile and dressed. They were damp—covered in sweat and salt water—but he felt better wearing them.

Looking at the door beside his torture room, he decided to see who it had held, if they were even identifiable. "Kash, bring me the body."

The dog dragged the corpse from the room, allowing Nikolai to study it. The height and build suited a male. Crouching down, he opened the eyelids. Bright blue eyes stared back at him. Sighing, Nikolai realized the mistake he made. Mihai had not betrayed him. They were both betrayed by the young couple. Though he wished to know why, no one was left to ask.

Only a silent house filled with the stench of death.

He went to the room where the tank was, recoiling at the sight. The tank was shattered on one side, and water was spread throughout the room, glass shards glittering. Oily black Siren blood blended into the water.

"Let's go find her, Kash."

Together, they walked through the halls to the front entrance. It was the smell that hit Nikolai first before he even walked around the corner.

A pile of bodies, all of Mihai's guests slaughtered, their throats slit. Blood stained the marble floor of the foyer.

"I bring so much death everywhere I go," Nikolai muttered, trying to tear his eyes away. Knowing he had to stay in this murder house for the next few hours until the sun set made his bones rattle.

"Run back, Nikolai."

The words came into his head like a migraine pulsing just behind his eyes.

"Find her, Nikolai," the Seer begged. *"Go back the way you came."*

Though Nikolai knew better than to trust any voice inside his head, he had no other choice.

Æsa was out there, and he would save her life, even if it cost him his own.

29

ÆSA

Æsa's second night with Zidler was the last show in Kæ'vale before they left for other parts of the world. Zidler had planned for them to have one final, albeit small, show before they took off back to the rest of the continent, far away from anyone who might be after them. Only those under the reign of the Mad King cared to hunt down Sirens anymore.

Æsa saw dozens of faces that night, all of them ogling her. Drunk off of ale and excitement, many of them did not hold back from banging on the glass to get a reaction from her, shouting rude things that she chose to ignore. She was not inside a tent this time, hidden away for only the highest paying customers. He took the risk of showing her off—one final peek before he whisked her away to another country.

Zidler's voice boomed with each new batch of people that walked right by all the other displays. They all went straight to her, though she gave them nothing. Not a flinch when they banged the glass, not a smile when they asked her politely, not even a bare of her teeth when they cursed her.

"Incredible! A real live Siren!" Zidler shouted. "Burned in the Great Wars, but a survivor who has prevailed against all the odds. In the clutches of a horrible bloodsucker, we saved her from a life of torture and gave her a home!"

"Make her sing!" Someone in the crowd shouted.

Æsa glanced up at that. Zidler might torture her in front of the crowd, even if that meant revealing to them that he was the real torturer. If they were leaving at sunrise, what did it matter if these few people knew the truth behind his circus? They would all turn a blind eye to her suffering because they enjoyed seeing these creatures. Just as Man turned a blind eye when Sirens were being killed in droves. Æsa recalled the little girl in the town she and Nikolai went through—perhaps they were already changing.

"How about a song, Æsa?" Zidler asked.

This request made Æsa grimace. To sing would be a violation of what she was: the Siren Song died a long time ago. Æsa knew that would never happen. She was the only Siren left. She would bite her own tongue off before she sang for them.

Zidler hobbled over to her, using his cane to disturb her. "Will you sing for us?"

They both knew the answer.

"She is shy, folks!"

Laughter.

When Sirens sang, the waters rippled under the vibrations of their collective voices, and a hymn of sorts would sound. Not like the voices of Man, boisterous and harsh, but flowing like the Sea itself. Entrancing—that was how Æsa remembered it. It was no wonder that sailors would once throw themselves to the Sea when the song started, coaxing them into the water.

They had no self-control.

While the crowd expected the serene hum and lull of the Siren Song, they got something else entirely—the distant thunder of footfalls followed by the distinct sound of screams. Amidst the confusion and panic from the crowd, Æsa knew what was coming for her. They had caught up. Nikolai had remained one step ahead and kept her safe from Eiríkur, but Zidler wanted to flaunt her for money and clout. His human desires were going to get them killed.

There could not have been a worse fate, Æsa decided, but at least death would come soon, and she would no longer have to mourn for Nikolai and Kashmir. She would no longer have to suffer at the hands of men who wanted her for so many horrible endeavors. She supposed her time had come. There were rumors that Eiríkur kept Árelía alive for months while he ate away at her. Her death would take time, but it would bring her peace.

By dying like Árelía, Æsa could be redeemed for what she had done to her Sisters.

The slaughter before her eyes was beautiful. She watched as all the circus-goers were brought down with swords. Throats slit, their blood shed—it was all being unraveled before her. Red and blue flags soared high, and horses stamped the ground, making it rumble furiously before charging through crowds who just wanted to escape.

Æsa watched through the charred glass as Zidler frantically hobbled away, his wounds hindering his movements. Making it no more than ten yards, he found himself face to face with a soldier. One upward slice and Zidler was opened from belly to throat. The ringleader fell to the blood-stained grass to be trampled by the crowd.

A woman clung to her skirt, lifting it so that she did not trip. Large, mismatched eyes looked up to meet Æsa's, and she pleaded silently with her. It was Fía. Æsa stared back with contempt. When a soldier appeared behind the woman, she did nothing to warn her. The soldier brought his sword down and sliced open the woman from shoulder to hip. Her scream lasted only seconds until she fell into the dirt, silenced.

"*Æsa,*" Nikolai's voice taunted her.

She clutched her hands over her ears; she did not need ghosts to haunt her.

"Æsa!" Nikolai shouted again, "Æsa, I'm here!"

She turned to look at the ghost, only to see that it was truly Nikolai. Her heart leaped into her throat. She covered her mouth, completely astounded by Nikolai's presence. He stood at the edges of the tank, fighting with the locks. He found a small piece of debris and used it to pick them. Time was ticking; soldiers were closing in on them as the circus-goers fled.

When the locks were off, Æsa pushed from underneath the lid, and with Nikolai's help, the heavy top opened. The hinges groaned. All these men, all this death—it was all for her. Nikolai reached his hands inside the tank and grabbed Æsa, who latched a little too tight to him as he began to lift.

"STOP!" A booming voice rang out—The Mad King himself.

They froze.

"Put her back," he commanded. With an entire army behind him, Nikolai was forced to obey. "Step away from the tank, Nikolai."

"How do you know my name?" Nikolai asked.

"I know a great many things. I am King, am I not?"

"I have no king."

"All of these people are dead. Do you know why?" Eiríkur asked. "They hid the location of a Siren from me. She is mine by law, and they were legally obligated to inform me of her whereabouts."

"I'm a bit of a rule breaker." Nikolai shrugged.

"Your punishment will match theirs in due time, Vampire."

"Don't hurt him." Æsa looked directly at the man who had killed and eaten her Sisters. "I will come with you should he be allowed to walk away."

"How righteous, just like Árelía. She held on longer than any other I ate...because she thought the longer she suffered, the longer the rest of them would have to escape." Eiríkur grinned. "However, I have promised him to someone else, I fear."

"Vlad! Bring in Otávia."

Nikolai went white as a ghost.

30

NIKOLAI

They brought the Seer through the sea of soldiers, strapped to a wooden device that wheeled along the blood-stained grass. Vlad walked beside her with his head held high and a hungry look in his eyes. When Nikolai spotted Otávia, his stomach turned. He wanted to drop to his knees and give up. It was his fault. He brought Vlad to Kæ'vale, and the Vampire followed him. Vlad turned Otávia in to Eiríkur to be tortured. He wondered how long it was before she was caught and captured.

The barmaid who helped guide him down the path to find Æsa was hardly recognizable, having been tortured for withholding the whereabouts of the Siren. Nikolai smelled the blood coming from her wounds —some of it was still fresh. In the firelight of the many torches, it was clear that they had done things to her that, should she live, would scar her forever.

"What does she have to do with this?" Nikolai asked. "I have seen this woman once."

"She is as guilty as the rest of them." Eiríkur spread his hand out, gesturing to the bodies surrounding them. "She guided you down the path to the Siren when she should have come straight to me. All this death could have been avoided."

Vlad stood with a wicked grin on his lips.

"Vlad," Nikolai greeted sourly.

"Nikolai." Vlad nodded at him. "Roman is very eager to see you."

"I'm sure he is."

Eiríkur walked up to Æsa, strolling right past Nikolai, knowing he could do nothing to stop him. If there was one thing that Eiríkur liked more than Siren flesh, it was power. His gloved hand touched the filthy glass, and he looked directly at Æsa. The tank stood two meters high, and she hovered just above him. When his blue eyes looked up at her, he expected her to shrink away. He appeared surprised when, instead, she looked at him serenely.

"Your name, it is Æsa?" He let the name roll off of his tongue in a way that made Æsa uncomfortable.

"How many of my Sisters did you devour?"

"Thousands." He narrowed his eyes. "Unfortunately, you may be my last."

"Do you know their names? Every one of them?"

"Of course not."

"Árelía, Sif, Eyvör, Ida, Íva, Kalla, Jara, Abela, Sera, Elea, Gytta, Líf—" Æsa stopped reciting the names and grabbed Eirikur's head on either side, slamming his forehead against the glass. Her mimicry of Nikolai's own fighting impressed him, though he was terrified for her.

Eiríkur stumbled away from her in shock, blood pouring from his nose.

"Luna, Silja, Sol, Maia, Mirja, Ora, Saga, Sæla, Tala, Rea, Torfa, Nenna, Nótt, Ófelía, Úrsúla—"

"That's enough!" He backhanded her, clearly disturbed by the fact that she knew every single one of her Sisters' names. Knocking her back revealed his shame.

She grinned at the Mad King. When she spat out her black blood, the Mad King fumed, unable to control his anger. He stomped his foot and turned on his heel away from the taunting Siren, and toward Nikolai.

Nikolai had to stand by and watch the two quarrel, wishing that he could throw himself at Eiríkur and beat his face to a pulp. Stock still and unable to do anything to protect Æsa, he felt utterly useless. Painful memories of finding his mother's corpse in the pond surfaced. He winced. Eiríkur stood in front of him, holding a beautifully crafted trident.

Árelía's trident.

He stood back, holding it to Nikolai's throat. Still sharp after all these years, the golden trident sparkled in the firelight. Feeling Æsa's eyes on him, Nikolai cast one look in her direction. If it was going to be the death of him, he wanted to lay his eyes on her just once more. White hair that always clung to her body, the scars of the burns, the scars of what she had overcome in her lifetime, those big amber eyes that were once filled with hope.

"I am sorry," he said to her. Death followed him everywhere he went, and it was his time to die. Maybe then the balance would right itself. He was sorry for failing Æsa, and he was sorry for leaving Kashmir behind.

Kashmir had done enough: he would not die for a lost cause.

Eiríkur grinned at Nikolai's defeat, then he raised the trident. Turning to his men, he raised a hand. "Burn the Witch."

"No!" Nikolai shouted.

He was restrained by two strong soldiers, who grabbed his arms and pinned them back.

Eiríkur paused where he stood, watching his soldiers build the pyre for the Witch. Turning ominously, his eyes landed on Nikolai again. Trident still in hand, Eiríkur walked over to him and grabbed his jaw.

"What will you do to stop me?" Eiríkur taunted.

"I—" Nikolai had no answer. He had never felt so weak in his entire life.

The Seer only began to curse in her language when they moved her battered body from the stretcher to the pyre. She bit and clawed and kicked to no avail, her tired body overwhelmed with the agony that she had endured since she last spoke to Nikolai. When her swollen eyes landed on him, however, there was no contempt in them. As if trying to ease the guilt that would remain until he died, Otávia revealed to Nikolai that she, too, chose to risk her life for Æsa.

Balance within yourself, Nikolai," she told him.

"When blood is spilled," he repeated, but he still didn't know what it meant. Her blood? Surely, her death would not bring a balance to anything. His own death would not bring balance, would it? His eyes glanced at Æsa. There could be balance if there were no Sirens left: Man would go back to the mundane.

He refused to believe it was Æsa's blood that needed to be spilled. Above all else, she had to come out of this alive.

Eiríkur still held Nikolai's jaw and forced him to watch as a soldier brought a torch to the bottom of the pyre. Sparks ignited the dry brush, and the fire was blazing in seconds. Bright, hot flames licked Otávia's feet, catching the torn skirt she wore. She held her tongue for as long as she could as the fire built up all around her, scorching her flesh. A deep howl of agony erupted through the fields when she cried out. It shook everyone who watched...except Eiríkur.

He smiled as she burned.

The minutes felt like hours before Otávia's head fell, the smoke killing her. The stench of human flesh and hair burning filled the air around them. When the Seer was entirely engulfed, Eiríkur released Nikolai's jaw. Trident raised again, he pressed it to Nikolai's chest.

The longest spike was so sharp it sliced easily through his shirt and layers of skin. Blood pooled over the front of his white shirt, and Nikolai glared at Eiríkur.

"You did not need to kill her," Nikolai said, his hands balled into fists.

"I would wait until the sun rises to kill you, Vampire, but I have a feast to prepare." His eyes flickered toward Æsa, and Nikolai snapped.

There was no point in being civil if they were all going to be dead by sunrise. Pulling his arm from the grip of the soldiers behind him, he stomped on the foot of one, then the other. They cried out in pain while Nikolai used his now free hands to pummel Eiríkur. Shoving the trident away, he felt adrenaline pump through his veins. He punched the twisted old man over and over, then wrapped both hands around his throat.

Eirikur's soldiers pulled Nikolai off within seconds. He knew that was the last fight he would ever be in. The Mad King raised the trident. "Vlad! Take your payment before I kill him right here and now!"

When there was no reply, Eiríkur turned, going rigid. Nikolai looked up with shock. Maybe it was not the end, but an even bigger threat loomed over them now.

31

ÆSA

Æsa hadn't noticed that more than half of the Mad King's men turned their weapons on him—her eyes had been on Nikolai the entire time. He had done everything he could to get her this far, and she would never blame him for how it turned out. Though she quivered with fear upon seeing everything fall apart so quickly and seeing the poor woman burned alive, she kept her eyes on Nikolai. He showed no fear, and she wondered if he was born brave or had learned it somewhere along the way.

Eiríkur spoke first, outraged by the sight of his men standing just behind Vlad. "What is the meaning of this?"

"It appears your men prefer my promises to your fear-mongering. For years, they waited for you to die. Now they're going to make sure you do." Vlad spoke casually, as if he had frequently organized military coups. Half of the army pitted against the other, at a stand-still for the moment.

"I order you to kill this man!" Eiríkur shouted.

"I am not a Man." Vlad grinned. "I might have lied when I said Vampires never break their promises; however, I did get you to the Siren. Turns out, my employer wants them both."

"This is an outrage! Kill him now! Kill any fool who dares turn his back on me!" Eiríkur shrieked like a child whose toy was taken from him.

"Traitors?" Vlad laughed a throaty laugh. "These men grovel at your feet, and they get nothing in return. I promised them something far more than you could ever offer."

"Enough of this. Bring me the Vampire's head!" Eiríkur waved a gloved hand then wiped the blood that dripped from his broken nose.

Men wearing the same colors attacked one another—men who had served together for most of their lives killed without a thought about their comrades. To Æsa, it was a collision of bodies, a swarm of shouting and metal upon metal. As it spread out over the field that was already littered with corpses like weeds sprouting in the garden, she realized that she had to take advantage of this distraction and escape her tank. She hoisted herself up—the drop was a long one—and she hesitated just long enough for a small scuffle of men to crash into the cage. It teetered, falling sideways off of the stand it was placed upon.

The ground came hard and fast, but Æsa used the force of the falling tank to launch herself free. When it hit the ground, it shattered. She braced herself, shielding her eyes from the onslaught of glass coming toward her. Opening her eyes, she realized that she was now in the brunt of the fighting. The soldiers appeared so swept up in killing the next person that her presence went quite unnoticed for the first time. She crawled along the grass to find Nikolai. Boots stomped all around her, and she had to roll away from being stepped on a handful of times.

In the commotion, she lost sense of which direction she needed to go. She rolled onto her stomach and looked around once she was hidden behind a cage that held the Wolf-Man's corpse. She scanned furiously for any sign of Nikolai.

Eiríkur had Árelía's trident pointed at him again.

"I planned to give you to Vlad, but now I'll have the satisfaction of killing you myself." Eiríkur raised the trident.

Æsa reached for the first piece of glass big enough to kill someone; it sliced her palm, but she felt nothing as she crawled over to stop Eiríkur. Nikolai appeared to be doing nothing to stop his own death, despite things having taken a turn for the better when Vlad turned against the Mad King. As Æsa crawled, her breath shuddering through her as she struggled along the blood-covered grass, she saw something from the corner of her eye that made her stop.

Eiríkur said something she didn't hear and then put his whole body into piercing the trident through Nikolai's chest. The high-pitched yelp that echoed through the field—louder than the yells of the soldiers and the clatter of metals colliding—was only matched by Nikolai's own screams.

Tears slid down Æsa's cheeks, rage filling her as she continued to crawl along. The sound of whimpering made her heart sink. The suffering—that was what made her break.

Both Kashmir's and Nikolai's.

The dog fell upon his side, heaving heavily as the trident was deep inside of his torso. Still alive, whimpering in pain, the dog's eyes searched for Nikolai. He dropped to the ground, his knees slamming hard against the grass, and his hands frantically hovered over Kashmir's body. He looked so startled, so broken, as he had no way of saving his best friend. Æsa had never seen Nikolai so disturbed, so unable to move or speak.

Æsa reached Eiríkur and grabbed his ankle. When he noticed her, he brought his boot back to kick her as she stabbed the shard of glass into his calf. He screamed in agony when she yanked down with the shard. The Mad King fell. With the shard in her grasp, she brought it down into his chest over and over again. She heard nothing except for the blood pulsing through her veins as she tasted what true war and fury felt like. Blood gushed from his chest, covering her.

"Árelía, Sif, Eyvör, Abela, Elea, Gytta, Ida, Luna, Maia, Mirja, Nenna, Saga, Sera, Nótt, Ófelía, Ora, Rea, Silja, Jara, Kalla, Sol, Íva, Líf, Sæla, Tala, Torfa, Úrsúla, Kashmir!" Æsa screamed the names of people she loved who Eiríkur had killed.

Blood spilled from his mouth as the light in his eyes went out like a candle in the wind.

She took in a shuddering breath, feeling arms wrap around her body. She knew they were Nikolai's, so she did not fight him as he took her away from the blood and battle.

32

INTERLUDE

The last throat had been slit.

Roman stepped gingerly along the blood-stained grass. Dawn was near, but Roman feared nothing. His long black coat swung in the wind, his gloved hands tucked in his pockets. Eyes upon the broken tank, he saw a faint shadow of his reflection and considered this for a moment. Head tipped, he released a deep sigh that he had been holding in.

"Roman." Vlad stood beside him. "We are very close now."

"Yes, we are." Roman's voice held a hint of joy, giving Vlad a moment of brief hope.

"They took off north, where Nikolai undoubtedly had a carriage with him. They won't get far—they must stop at a body of water." Vlad glanced over at the abundance of horses at their disposal. They could chase after Nikolai and catch him within a few hours.

"You've done quite well, Vladimir." Roman's bright blue eyes looked at the Nightwalker, aged with stress lines. "You have done *almost* everything, my loyal compatriot."

"May I ask, why did you not uphold the promise to the soldiers?" Vlad gestured to the heaps of bodies on the ground. All were promised the life of a Vampire if they turned against their king, but all were delivered death at the hand of Ivan instead. Ivan was currently double-checking the bodies and feasting freely upon them.

"They were turncoats." Roman's voice peaked halfway through, his voice holding a playful edge that made him all the more frightening.

"So," Roman continued, "my brother is not in my clutches like you promised—"

"Roman," Vlad began to defend himself. "There was so much going on, it would have been impossible to subdue him."

"Impossible for you, maybe." Roman turned to face Vlad. "Unfortunately for you, I do not accept failure twice. You have failed me before, and I allowed you a second chance. Was that not generous of me?"

"Roman, please..." Vlad raised his hands, then dropped to his knees. "I beg you..."

"Oh, beg—beg if it is what you want to be remembered for." Roman sneered. He lived for this, breaking people down until they were nothing, pushing them as far as they would go. And Vlad was so easy to break.

Vlad shut his mouth, though he was visibly shaking.

After removing his lamb-skin gloves, Roman reached over with muscular hands and long fingernails, sharp enough to penetrate skin. Gently gripping his jaw, he lifted his head up so that he could look into his eyes. Leaning down, he kissed Vladimir on either cheek. When he stood straight again, he nodded his approval of Vladimir's new-found bravery and then snapped his neck. Muscles flexing, he held the dead man for a moment before laying his body on the ground among the others.

Roman cracked his neck from side to side. Turning where he stood, he spotted Ivan sauntering through the bodies. He paused occasionally to roll one over, making sure no one was still alive, hiding beneath the corpse of another. They had been through enough war to know people were cowards. When he made it to Roman, he was covered head to toe in blood.

Ivan wiped blood from his mouth, his grin spreading wide as he looked at Vlad. He stepped over the body and asked Roman: "So, what now, Brother?"

Roman stared ahead, beyond the heaps of bodies, out to where Nikolai had fled. "We find our baby brother."

33

ÆSA

They were racing against time, and the horses moved their feet at such velocity that the very Earth below them quaked. The carriage on the back rattled mightily, and Æsa clutched her own blood-covered body to fight off her anguish. Though she had single-handedly killed The Mad King, she felt no joy or satisfaction for what she had done. How could she, when Kashmir lay dead on the field with so many others?

They could not even take his body with them.

When, at last, the horses began to quit, their muscular bodies growing tired under Nikolai's expectations, Æsa opened the small window at the front of the carriage. Noticing his hunched-over shoulders, she spoke.

"Nikolai, we must stop," she commanded him in a soft voice.

"No." He beckoned the horses on again.

"The sun has nearly risen," Æsa cried. There was no tank in the back of the carriage anymore. She wouldn't survive a full day without water, and Nikolai would die if he was out there when dawn broke.

"I can't stop!" He shouted at her, voice dripping with acrimony. "He's dead because of me. I can't lose you too! I'm getting you there!"

"The night is gone, Nikolai. Stop the carriage!" She screamed back at him, even though she knew that his anger was not directed to her. Grief did terrible things to even the best of people. "Getting yourself killed will not bring him back!"

He slammed the window shut to ignore her.

Æsa scowled. Instead of opening the window again to continue shouting at him, she crawled to the back of the carriage and fumbled with the latch, pushing the doors wide. They banged against the sides of the carriage. Up above, the sky was too light, but she needed Nikolai to be safe—she needed him alive at all costs. Grabbing a glass bottle, she threw it to the ground. It crashed loudly against the rocky terrain.

The horses slowed. Nikolai was surely listening since the doors rattled open. Their thundering hoofbeats would dampen the sound of the glass, but she knew he heard it. They picked up speed again as he veered the carriage over. The bumpy terrain made the wheels groan and creak as though they were ready to give up under the strain. It was clear to Æsa that he was going to push them to the last moment possible.

She threw another bottle—this one amber-colored—and the carriage came to a jerking stop. The horses grunted their sounds of approval. Æsa heard Nikolai hop off the carriage and stomp to the back. She was seated out the edge of the carriage, the doors wobbling slightly in the cold wind. When he came around the back of the carriage, he looked furious. Æsa surely looked the same. Arms crossed over her chest, she stared him down, challenging him.

"We have to stop for the day," she told him like a mother scolding her disobedient child.

"Do you understand who is coming?" He ran his hands frantically through his hair, "No, of course you don't! How could a *Siren* who gave up her safety for *nothing* understand anything I've gone through?"

She slapped him hard, leaving a giant red mark that would sting for hours. She leaned forward with a scowl that put his own to shame. "Don't you dare say I do not understand! Thousands of my Sisters died for me. For me, Nikolai! That is what happened back there—Kashmir died for *you*. Because he loved you!

"You may not care about whether the sun rises and you die today, but I do! Without you, I have no friends, no family...no home. Without you, I die too. But with you... Nikolai, let me be your home." She didn't realize she was holding his hands in hers until that moment. She clutched tighter.

Like a glass that had been dropped, Nikolai suddenly fell apart. He leaned forward, clutching Æsa in his grasp as though she was the only thing that could keep him whole. The embrace was quickly reciprocated as she wrapped her arms around his large frame. She nuzzled into him, smelling his scent, a combination of soap and sweat, blood and dirt.

"I was supposed to protect him," he muttered through tears.

"And he, you," Æsa reminded him. "His life was to protect you, Nikolai."

Even as the carefully selected words came off of her tongue, Æsa remembered a time when her Sisters had protected her. She understood why they fought for her life, even if it hardly amounted to anything. But they had also been fighting for their own lives; each and every one of them faced the Great Wars head-on with the knowledge that the chances of them being killed were extremely high. Even if Æsa had not interfered, Eyvör and the others would likely still have been captured and killed.

It didn't absolve her pain, but the knowledge that they fought for themselves as much as for her eased it.

Nikolai pulled from her embrace, looking her in the eyes. "I'm going to get you there."

"How many of my Sisters have you saved?"

"Three," he told her. Without any other warning, he lifted her from the back of the carriage. There was water close, and now Æsa knew why he veered off earlier. Nikolai's pushing had gotten them close enough. Time was running short. Despite his desire to go further ahead to escape what was following them, the horses and Æsa were no longer up to the challenge. He began walking through a field of scraggly grass that all looked gray in the fading night. When the water was in sight, he added, "I lost the fourth."

"Who?"

"Her name was Sif. You mentioned her," his voice wavered.

"What happened to her?"

"She saved my life." He placed Æsa in the murky pond water. It was all they had, and she would not complain. Around them, there was nothing but lichen-covered rock.

Æsa's heart thumped. Though she had assumed Sif perished years ago, she, too, had known Nikolai. He had once held her in his arms like he held Æsa. He gave Sif the chance of survival, even if he had not succeeded. A brave Siren, Sif had fought since the day the Great Wars began. But she had never boasted about killing Man, the ships she tore apart, the terrified faces of those she drowned. She expressed that not all of Man was vile; most followed orders without question. Sif had been humble, brave. Æsa wished she were those things.

"Hunters closed in on us, a party of two dozen," Nikolai explained, seated on the shore of the pond, his boots soaked. "We were so close to safety. I did everything I could to hold them at bay, hoping Sif would crawl away, hoping she would do anything to save herself. Her life was worth more than mine. But she fought by my side, and I watched—"

He broke off as if the memory haunted him like so many others. As if he didn't want Æsa to know what happened, how badly he had failed her Sister. How he could fail her, too. She knew that at this point, with every-thing that Nikolai had done, even if she died, he did not fail. Not to her. Not when everyone was trying to kill her, and he was to die to save her.

She encouraged him to go on with a gentle nod, her eyes wide.

"She took down at least half of them. Saved my life four times that night." He shuddered.

Æsa knew that look in his eyes, the fear. Fear of a memory could be worse than fearing what was in the future. You could not change a memory.

After a moment, he finally added, "They cut her head off."

Æsa covered her mouth, bile threatening to spill from her. She'd seen the corpses of her Sisters—she'd seen them burned and scarred, dead and floating above the shore and completely obscuring the sun above. But the thought of Sif fighting back as they brought down a sword or knife to her ivory throat... It was too much for Æsa.

"I saw red after that," Nikolai said. "I woke up from a frenzy covered in blood, but I never really woke up from that nightmare."

Æsa clutched his hand, steadying herself by grasping onto his strength. "You are a gift, Nikolai."

As he looked at her again, she felt a twist deep inside of her. Something began falling from the sky—not rain, something much lighter. Reaching her hand up, she touched what she first thought was ash. But the ice-cold flakes did not smell like singed flesh and burning wood. They stuck to her wet hair, freezing it. Looking up at the harmless cold ash, she stuck out her tongue and caught one on her tongue. It chilled her, and she smiled.

"The Snow Maiden makes her grand entrance," Nikolai mumbled before rising to his feet. He bid no farewell with words, only a broken glance at Æsa that held something more, something that warmed her.

34

NIKOLAI

The carriage began to fall apart under the strain. Nikolai was desperate to move quickly to keep ahead of those chasing them, but they were slower now. He had to fix two wheels of the carriage, and he feared he wouldn't be able to return with it. Nikolai had little doubt in his ever-worried mind that Roman had servants to allow him to travel day and night. Without Kashmir at his side anymore, there was no safety for them. They were close to a place where Æsa would live out her days.

Nikolai didn't know what was coming after that. However, he had a few ideas.

He had considered turning himself over to his brother once, and for all to end this ongoing dread he called a life. His brother was so close now, and he could almost feel Roman's long fingers wrapping around his throat, strangling him. But each time he glanced into the back of the carriage and saw the glimmer of Æsa's tail in the lantern light, he realized he still had something to live for. Just because things were hard for him did not mean he had to die. After he lost Sif, he had gone six years searching for another Siren to save, and not once had he considered turning himself into Roman and accepting death.

Glancing at the carriage, he knew he had something to fight for.

Some*one* to fight for.

He shook the reins to encourage the horses to move faster.

The snow slowed them, thick blankets obscuring the ground. The carriage wheels seized, sinking into the drifts. The brute strength of the horses prevailed, and they pushed through without complaint. Each huff of breath left clouds in the air, each step muffled by the cold snow. A communal silence wrapped itself around them.

Nikolai lost count of how many nights it took to get to the safety of the cove.

The beautiful landscape was dark when they arrived, carefully navigating the sloping fields. It was rocky, tough on the carriage and the horses alike. The peninsula reached far into the ocean, with great walls of rock leading down to the water. Nikolai remembered the route like the back of his hand, passing by landmarks that he had made note of when he saved his first Siren. Now, he passed by them with dread, fearful that they might be dead now. He couldn't simply dump Æsa in a cove and bid her farewell if there were no Sirens left. The anguish it would cause her would be too much.

He had no plan after that, so he tried not to think about it. He did have one thing to ask of her after all of this but wondered if he could get himself to say the words.

"They're alive," he told himself in a grumble, trying to rid his mind of all the recent deaths.

A raven swooped low enough to make the horses rear in shock. Nikolai shouted at them to soothe them. "Whoa, whoa!"

They stomped their feet as the raven elegantly glided away. Nikolai shot a glare at the beast, a sickening feeling twisting inside of him. It wasn't the same raven he saw when he was tracking Æsa or the one at the safe house. It couldn't be. Ravens did not follow people.

At least, ordinary ones did not.

When the path to the water came into sight, he focused on the task at hand, pushing thoughts of the bird from his head. He stopped the carriage and untied the horses so that they could roam freely. With his hand on the velvet-smooth nose of the larger horse, he rested his forehead against the beast. When he closed his eyes, he imagined it was Kashmir.

Spooked by the night, the horses lingered close, afraid to venture too far from the person who had cared for them. As they grazed, eyes flickering nervously up at the movement to their left, Nikolai opened the back of the carriage.

"We're here," his voice cracked.

Æsa reached her arms out, and Nikolai recoiled slightly when he realized her hand was crusted in her blood. Holding it gently, he silently reached behind her to bandage it up. A dash of the last of the vodka—his eyes squinted in playful blame—and some clean cloth, and she was ready to get out of the stifling carriage and into the Sea once again.

He carried her in silence. Both of them realized what this meant—this was the end of their time together. Though it had been short, they both overcame so much and grew closer together than they ever would have imagined at the start. He felt the bruise upon his shoulder when she rested her head upon it, her arms tight around his neck. The black sand slipped under his worn-down boots, and he nearly collapsed, sliding for a moment before getting his footing again. Holding her a little bit tighter as he maneuvered down the rest of the path, he realized how badly he didn't want to let go.

In front of them was the dark water, and the sound of a waterfall in the distance filled the silence. Above them, the sky was covered in gray clouds that obscured the stars. But as Nikolai grew closer to the water, he smelled something rancid, something that made his nostrils flare and his taste buds tang. Æsa did not smell it, but she felt his tension and glanced nervously around them.

Wading into the water, waist-deep now, Nikolai began to discover what it was. He released Æsa, though she remained close, distraught as they both came to the same realization. Nikolai ran his hand through the water, and when it came back up, it was black as night itself. Thick like molasses, the top layer of the water was darkened and stained with Siren blood; the smell had been masked by Æsa's own blood, the color hidden by the dark of the night.

"He's here." A shiver ran down Nikolai's spine. He had no idea if there were any Sirens left, but he knew that Æsa had to get far, far away. "Swim, Æsa. Get away from here!"

Æsa looked at him, shattered that they had to part this way, but she dove deep into the bloody water, disappearing under the surface. Nikolai turned, noticing the two tall figures clad in all black on the shore. He had not seen them in his distraction over giving up Æsa.

"Brother!" Roman called, his voice echoing off the great rocks that made up the cove. He spread his arms wide. "You would not come home to us, so we came to you."

"How did you find me?"

"You do not seem joyous to see us, Little Brother," Ivan said, a teasing tone in his voice.

"Because I am not." Nikolai scowled, hands clenching.

"I understand you have much to be upset about." Roman clicked his tongue. "But we are family, and family must make amends."

"I'll come with you." Nikolai knew it was time to face this once and for all. "But tell me, how did you find me?"

"Really, Brother, you are naïve." Roman chuckled. "This cove, this field, these rocks... They look just like home. You are nothing if not predictable."

Nikolai gaped at him, taken aback by his answer. It could not possibly be the truth. His thoughts trailed to the raven—it was her familiar. Roman's Witch.

Nothing was safe from Roman: anything connected to Nikolai would be found and destroyed. He had taken everything Nikolai loved away from him. He would not let him take Æsa.

"Ivan." Roman clicked his tongue again. "Fetch me the Siren. I'll handle our brother."

"No!" Nikolai trudged through the water, desperate to get away from the scent of death, desperate to protect Æsa. He heard splashing in the distance and saw the evidence of a net securing the cove. His brothers were one step ahead of him. He charged at Roman when he finally made it to the shore, his brother meeting him halfway. Roman brought his right arm back, slamming his fist hard into Nikolai's jaw.

He fell back into the water, and Roman dropped down on top of him, shoving his head beneath the surface. Nikolai clamped his mouth shut, forcing air out through his nose. Clutching his brother's wrists, he tried to fight him off. Pinned under the heavy weight of his brother, he couldn't use his strength to force him off. He had nothing left, not even the desire to save Æsa gave him the strength to overcome Roman—he was always the better fighter.

Nikolai realized he was going to die just like his mother. He was going to drown in the blood of the Sirens he could not save. He stopped fighting. Just as his consciousness faded, Roman pulled him up from the water.

35

ÆSA

Æsa woke in a metal basin; the rope wounds that covered her head-to-fin stung in the water. Not nearly as large as Mihai's tank, this one was oval-shaped and too short for her body to be vertical. Instead, she let her tail sink under the water and rested her head against the basin. Æsa's head swam, exhausted from fighting her way through the ropes in the cove, then manhandled by Nikolai's brother, Ivan. She noticed she was in a large room with bare walls, the windows boarded up.

What stood out to her most was the one chair and the menacing presence occupying it. He was clad in black, hands resting in his lap. Simply seated there, doing nothing violent. Yet the threat he carried with him lingered, filling the room.

"You're Roman."

"Ah, you've heard of me!" He clapped his gloved hands together excitedly. "Good things, I do hope."

"I wouldn't say that."

"Hmm." He frowned. He looked quite a bit older than Nikolai—perhaps ten years older—with creases around his eyes and lips when his expression changed. His hair was slicked back and shaved down on the sides to show his tattoos. He leaned forward and began removing his gloves. "Nikolai likes to cast himself as the victim. He loves the attention."

"From what I have heard, you are the one who likes the attention."

Underneath his black lamb-skin gloves, his hands were scarred and tattooed with long fingernails. Grime coated them—Siren blood, most likely. Æsa did not recoil from him. She eyed him, wondering why he decided he wanted her as well. Nikolai, she understood, but why her? Perhaps he thought the taste of Siren flesh would be worth trying.

But she suspected it was something far more sinister than that.

"I do not wish to hurt you, my dear." His voice was one that one might hear mocking in the distance as they lay dying—one that soothed and calmed while causing pain. He shifted slightly. "You are here for a reason."

"What reason?"

"I may need you to help show my brother the way back onto the correct path. If he refuses to return, his only other option is death. A King who cannot control his kingdom is weak. I cannot appear weak."

Roman stood up, smiling wryly when Æsa flinched. Grabbing the chair, he dragged it along the floor and flipped it around. He straddled it, resting his arms on the back. He cocked his head to the side.

"Tell me, will you help me?"

Æsa leaned over the edge of the basin and spat on the ground in answer. Striking fear into hearts was something he clearly took pride in, and so she would not show him fear.

"You killed your mother," Æsa snarled at him, leaning over the glass and letting her eyes bore into his blue ones, which were exactly like Nikolai's.

Roman grinned. "Is *that* what he told you?"

"Yes." Æsa believed it; why would Nikolai lie to her?

"Did he tell you she begged for death because of him?"

"No... He..."

"Ah!" Roman clapped his hands together again. "Just as I thought, Nikolai plays the tortured victim, yet never brings up the blood on his hands."

"He would do nothing without reason. He is just," Æsa insisted.

"Oh, he may very well be." Roman nodded, then stopped with his eyes on Æsa, digging under her flesh with that stare. He continued, "After the war that brought us greatness, our lifestyle bore down on his weak shoulders. He longed to kill himself—he tried many times."

Æsa tried to look away, but his cold stare held her as though she was hypnotized by the blue. Roman spoke of wars that brought greatness. How could a war possibly be great? A Great War had killed all of her kind. Men who pined for war were evil.

"Unable to take his own life, because he was too weak for that, he decided to kill our father. For he was the one who created us, created him. And Nikolai, he is a killer. He may not have the strength to kill himself, but he certainly succeeded with our father. We found him beaten to death, sliced open from belly to throat, hanging from a tree." Roman sighed.

Æsa could not tell if he was lying or simply revealing a truth that Nikolai withheld. Could she blame him, though? Æsa did not know what Nikolai's father was like.

"You see, The Brotherhood was, and is, hanging together by a thread. If anyone caught wind that one of us had gone insane, it would all crumble. I am trying to stop another war, you see.

"Nikolai needed space to clear his head and wash our father's blood from his hands. But stains like that, nothing removes those from our hearts and our hands. We asked for his return. We forgave him for killing our father. He was never much of one to begin with. But Nikolai refused to recover, refused to accept his place in the Brotherhood. We needed him.

"You see, after he killed our father, our mother seemed to lose her mind. She could not cope with family turmoil—she never could—and he vowed to keep her safe and sane until she died. Nikolai thought he was doing the right thing, but he was so blinded by his own righteousness... Well, the truth was, she was terrified of Nikolai. He had killed her husband, the father of her three children. Living with him was like living with a monster. He thought he was protecting her, but he was trapping her within her own home, her own mind."

"You're lying." Æsa hoped he was, at least.

"When we returned to fetch our baby brother, we found her alone." Roman continued as if Æsa hadn't spoken at all. "She begged us to free her from the prison Nikolai kept her in. We offered her shelter with us, but she wanted nothing to do with her family anymore. So, Ivan offered her a mercy killing, and she accepted death with open arms.

"So, now that you know, do you still think Nikolai is as good as he claims?" Roman inquired, leaning forward again with wide eyes.

"We've all done horrible, regretful things in the past. What I know is that Nikolai saved my life time and time again. He is good to his core—the past does not matter. What he did for me, for Kashmir... That is all that matters to me," Æsa responded at last. After everything Nikolai did for her, she would not believe Roman's words were true. "I will do nothing you ask of me."

"Ah, stubborn," Roman muttered. "Very well. I shall have Nikolai brought in to see you."

Confused, Æsa cocked her head to the side. There was nothing good about the way Roman spoke and acted, and she did not understand the things he said or what he meant.

Roman rose from the chair, knocking it over in a concentrated rage. With three broad steps along the floor, he reached the door. He glanced once over his shoulder and sighed. "It's a shame. I do think you are quite beautiful. You remind me a bit of my mother, only stronger. I will be sad to see you go."

Æsa trembled.

"Ivan, bring our baby brother in," Roman shouted down the hall.

When Nikolai and Ivan appeared in her line of sight, she noticed the striking resemblance between the brothers. They would have all been very handsome men, but stress and war had made them all look perpetually tired. Ivan was the most handsome, Æsa realized. He looked far less stressed but far crueler, with a scar beside his right eye.

Nikolai had one swollen eye, bulging and black, obscuring the beautiful blue. Held by his collar, he looked meek and distraught. Æsa wished to call out to him that it would be okay. They would be together for a while before whatever came next.

"Let's see how long it takes for Nikolai to break his code and kill himself once and for all," Roman taunted.

Ivan threw Nikolai in, locking the door behind them with a gut-wrenching click of the key. Nikolai stumbled, vomit and blood on his shirt collar.

36

NIKOLAI

An impenetrable silence filled the small room. Bearing the heavy weight of knowledge, Nikolai couldn't bring himself to look at Æsa knowing his brother's plans. Despite the desperate urge to check on her wounds—old and new—he relocated to the corner of the room and refused to face her. Even feeling her eyes burning through his shroud of disregard for her, he kept himself tucked away.

"Nikolai," Æsa spoke softly, the lull of her beautiful voice calling to him.

Her voice felt like a hallucination—too beautiful to be in this dark, ugly world.

He lolled his head to the side so that one ear was pressed against the bone of his shoulder, drowning out the sound by placing his hand over the other. Nothing he had done had kept her safe, and now she knew his secrets, his sins. Even though Nikolai knew she likely didn't believe what Roman had told her, he knew it was true.

He lied to Æsa about protecting her; he lied to her about his own mother. He was truly a monster, born that way. From the earliest memories he had of killing to the ones that ripped him apart from the inside to the ones that had felt good, Nikolai knew he was nothing more than a murderer.

Nikolai couldn't force himself to look at her, not after what Ivan told him. When Roman and Ivan arrived at the cove, the Sirens mistook them for him. They rose to greet the man who saved some of them but instead found themselves face-to-face with a great evil. Ivan was relentless as he killed them: seven died by his hand that night. Ivan brought their heads to show him.

His fault.

"Nikolai," she called again, only this time there was weight to it—not anger, but something similar.

Contempt?

Betrayal?

Disappointment?

"All," Nikolai said to himself.

"Nikolai, look at me," she screamed at last.

Throughout their whole journey, she had only yelled at him once. That was after Kashmir died, which seemed so far away now, though the pain still lingered.

He was already losing his mind.

"Nikolai!"

"What?" he screamed back at her, shifting his body like a feral creature that had been chained and beaten its whole life. His eyes were filled with dread and anger, but not toward her. He steadied himself with his hand, placing it on the floor and grimacing toward Æsa. In his moment of rage, he had overreacted; only when he focused on her did he feel calm. There was pity and something else in her eyes. Nikolai took a deep breath and shuddered out, "*What?*"

"What's next?" she asked, somehow still filled with hope.

"Next?" He raised his eyebrows. "There's nothing. I failed."

Her eyes narrowed into vicious slits. "I thought that my time had ended when Zidler purchased me. I thought it again when you stole me from his circus. And again when Fía and Davi betrayed us, then when Eiríkur appeared. When the killing started. When Kashmir died." She took a deep breath. "But when I saw your brothers at the ocean last night, I knew it wasn't the end."

"That's where you're wrong, Æsa; you don't know what my brothers are capable of." Nikolai leaned against the wall so hard that organs jostled inside of him. His stomach rumbled. "They have been hunting me for years. They have had *years* to decide what they will do with me, and I deserve every last ounce of the punishment they will mete out. You don't, and yet here you are. You don't know what they are going to make me do to you."

"Tell me about your mother."

He furrowed his brows, confused, but felt compelled to do as she asked. It was as if she had an allure, not unlike the one Vampires had on Man. He held his hand out, showing her the faded old ink of the lily tattoo. "Her name was Lily. You know the rest."

"I know what you told me, and I know what Roman told me."

Nikolai scowled when his brother's name came off her lips.

"Did you know how she felt?"

He shook his head. "I had no idea she feared me. I didn't believe Roman when he told me after he killed her. I lost my mind once before. I couldn't fix what needed fixing...and I lost sight of myself."

"You're not a bad person."

"Maybe not now, but I will be soon." Nikolai slid down the wall, facing away from Æsa. Facing her would mean telling her the truth, all of it, and he couldn't bear to reveal the truth. Not to her, not to himself.

He was disgusting.

He was greedy.

He was no different from Man.

For a day, Nikolai spoke nothing to Æsa despite her pleas, her kind words, her softness, and her understanding way of looking at him. It was near impossible to avoid looking at her while she stared, whispering to him, and even more so when she began to give up. She had lost weight, even though she had food. She wasn't eating. Nikolai found himself looking at her only when she was asleep, finding that even more painful.

To gaze upon what she might look like dead.

He knew that it would not be peaceful. Her death would not be pain-free—she would not simply slip away and die as she slept. No, it would be bloody, it would... It would be like the ones in the cove. An image of her head removed from her body, Ivan holding it up by her hair.

By the second day, Nikolai was sure he was losing his mind.

When was the last time he ate? He could not remember.

Fía's parents. Then, some stale blood along the final leg of the journey to the cove.

Fía's mother had been over a week ago, his last full meal. The stale blood had been days ago. Three? Four? Nikolai clutched his head, his nails digging into his scalp, breaking the skin. He stared at the blood. Even though it would give him no nutrients but perhaps peace of mind, he tasted the blood desperately. It tasted like iron, metallic and bitter, but it was something.

He wondered, glancing over his hunched shoulder like some cave creature, if killing her would be the merciful thing to do. If he did it in the most peaceful way possible, he could prevent the inevitable. He could snap her neck; it would be fast.

But no, he knew then that if he were too near Æsa with any intent other than what Roman wanted, his brother would put a stop to it. There was a flap on the door: he was watching. Not that Nikolai believed he could ever harm Æsa—the very thought of killing her was abhorrent.

Nikolai roared, a howl coming from his lips as he realized there was no escaping this. He had failed, and he wanted to crumble into dust. His bones ached; he felt the throbbing pulse of his blood—

No, he felt Æsa's blood pulsing just across the room.

Another yell.

"Nikolai!" She screamed at him. She held out her arm.

Nikolai stared at her, petrified at what she was going to do. "No, no, no," he mumbled.

"Just take my blood—" She brought her wrist to her mouth.

"Æsa, stop!" He brought himself to his unsteady feet. Stumbling as he tried to reach her in time, he cursed himself for being so weak. Every bone and muscle ached; he needed sustenance.

Finally crossing the room, he grabbed her arm away from her mouth, but his hand came back sticky and black.

They both stared at the blood. Even her blood, thick and rancid as it was, tempted him. Saliva dripped from his lips, and he could not tear his eyes away from his own hands. The blood still pulsed from her fresh wound—he could hear it.

Gush.

He shuddered, shook to his core. His eyes felt as though they were bulging from their sockets. He brought his hand to his lips, just a centimeter away.

When his eyes finally tore from the blood, and he looked at Æsa, he shook his head.

"They'll kill you," he mumbled, even if she didn't understand.

Dipping his hands into the water of her tank, he washed the blood from them.

With temporary sanity, he walked to the door, banging hard with both hands.

"I won't do it," he said to whoever was on the other side, knowing his defection would be relayed back to Roman.

He stood defiant, waiting.

37

ÆSA

Roman walked in a few minutes later, the great door swinging open. Æsa watched as he strode in, confidence in each movement. After years of searching for his brother, he finally had him in his clutches to toy with as he found fitting. Roman glanced at Æsa for a brief moment before settling his gaze on Nikolai.

"Starvation is not becoming of you, brother," he said to Nikolai. "Your complexion is just dreadful."

Nikolai didn't speak.

Roman continued as though Æsa wasn't right there next to them. "Æsa offered you her blood, Nikolai. It is rude to turn down such generosity."

"You know what would happen," Nikolai growled.

"Ah yes, I am very aware." Roman nodded and flashed a grin toward Æsa. He removed strips of fabric from his coat pocket. "But it appears she is not..."

Roman turned on his heel, causing the floor below him to squeal unpleasantly. What was far more unpleasant was the way that he looked at her, those bright eyes so full of wickedness. Two strides, and he stood beside her basin. Æsa had not hesitated to break Eiríkur's nose, but she dared not move in front of Roman. How could a villain who had struck

163

fear in her heart since she was a child seem so small compared to this Vampire standing before her now?

"Æsa." His eyelids lowered when he said her name, as though it were euphoric for him to speak it with Nikolai standing right there. Roman was brave, turning his back on his brother. When he beckoned for her wounded arm, she did not deny him: it may be the small actions that kept Nikolai alive. She held it out to him, and he studied her wound with startling tenderness. "Nikolai told you that I killed our mother but neglected to mention that she wished for death because she was terrified of him. Did he ever tell you that he wanted to kill me?"

"He ran from you," she whispered.

"Or that he killed his best friend? Why, Nikolai has killed more people he loved than anyone I know." Roman began wrapping her wound, his touch gentle. "There was one more thing that he forgot to tell you."

"Roman, don't," Nikolai cautioned.

Roman glanced over his shoulder and grinned wickedly. "Why don't you tell her then, Little Brother?"

"There is nothing to tell—"

"Oh, she will find out!" Roman shouted. When he turned back to Æsa, he grimaced, looking strikingly like Nikolai. "Nikolai did not save you because of that pathetic myth he doesn't even believe—"

"About drowned women?" Æsa whispered. Eyes on Nikolai, she hardly raised her voice another octave. "Nikolai?"

He met her gaze, saying nothing.

Roman's voice was full of mockery. "You see? He is too ashamed to admit it, because the truth behind why he stole you in the first place is degrading."

"It's not," Nikolai argued. "And I did not ask her."

Roman rolled his eyes. "Æsa, my dear, you are a weapon."

Puzzled, she opened her mouth to speak but did not know what to say or what to ask. Shutting her pale lips, she stared hard at Roman. She would not play his game, but she would listen to what she was told.

"Siren blood is poisonous to Vampires," Roman said.

Æsa pondered this, trying to sort it all out. But all she realized was that when Roman locked the two of them in the room together with the intent to starve Nikolai, it was to force his hand and break him in two ways. Roman wanted Nikolai to kill her, drink her blood, and thus, end his own life.

"Nikolai wanted to help you so you would owe him a debt. Then he could poison me like a coward." Roman sneered. "Isn't that right, Little Brother?"

"No...I..." His words fell apart like a sand sculpture at the incoming tide.

"Not for our mother. Not for the other murdered and drowned women. Not out of the goodness of your heart. Not to atone for the crimes you've committed, and you have committed so many. No, Nikolai —you did this only to get revenge."

"Nikolai," Æsa said, her soft voice cutting through Roman's shouting. "Is this true?"

"Yes." He watched her eyebrows knit together in confusion. "Revenge was the reason I started saving Sirens, but..." he trailed off when he saw Æsa's face fall.

Roman grinned from ear to ear. "You foiled my plans, unfortunately. You were stronger than I thought, Nikolai. However, that does not mean I cannot have some fun while you're still alive."

"Just let her go." Nikolai's voice was weak. He trembled from hunger and fear.

"Did you ask the others?" Æsa asked him, still contemplating the fact that her blood could be used as a weapon against the Vampire standing in front of her. A Vampire whom Nikolai told her believed in all the myths surrounding Sirens.

Both Roman and Nikolai looked up at her.

"Did you ask the others for their blood?" she asked again.

"No. I never had the courage. It meant I would have to face it, to go back." Nikolai's eye flickered to Roman briefly before landing back on Æsa.

"Were you going to ask for mine?"

"I hadn't decided," he admitted. "You seemed like the first one...the first one who might have actually given it to me. You were the first one I told about—" His breath hitched. "My mother."

Roman scoffed. "It's time for you to get over Mother."

Nikolai looked at Æsa, her eyes boring into him. Not to show she was upset with this new piece of information—his motive made very little difference to her. He had risked his life numerous times to save her; giving him a little bit of blood to kill his brother would not have been an issue for her. It was the least she could have done. He'd earned her trust. Roman thought that Æsa would think Nikolai evil for what he had done, but he hadn't been there when Nikolai tended her wounds, fought for her life, carried her to the ocean, made her laugh, and gave her hope.

She hoped he understood that when she looked at him that way.

Roman stepped toward the door, knocking twice. The locks and bolts were undone again, and Ivan entered the room. Head nearly shaved with tattoos along the side, Ivan was the most frightening of them. All of them were handsome, but the looks on each of their faces told different stories.

Roman's was power.

Ivan's was cruelty.

Nikolai's was something else entirely.

38

NIKOLAI

Ivan grinned, his eyes on Æsa.

The twisted way he looked at her made something inside of Nikolai twist. He had no power here, no way of stopping whatever thoughts Ivan had running through that disturbed mind of his. Nikolai had seen up close what Ivan was capable of doing without losing sleep. He dreamed of torture, of pain. It was he who should have been born Pure Blooded, not Nikolai.

"Ivan thinks we might be able to make ourselves immune to Siren Blood. Isn't that right, Brother?" Roman looked at Ivan with a love between them that had never extended to Nikolai. There had always been jealousy because of Nikolai's blood status. "Our Sister Torenia learned a great deal about your kind."

Nikolai stared at him, long and hard. He had no doubt the raven was Torenia's—the Witch Roman relied on to find him here in Kæ'vale.

"Of course, we would have to drain small doses, keep her alive as we test it upon lower Nightwalkers... The process would be quite long. I imagine we will have her in our clutches for a very long time. Oh, and Nikolai, I thought it would be appropriate to have you as our first subject?"

"You know my answer." Nikolai didn't realize his hands were balled,

167

his nails digging into his palm. Blood spilled, dripping from his finger-tips to the cold wooden floor below. "Let her go, and I will come willingly to whatever you beckon me to."

"But I already have you," Roman placed his hand on Nikolai's cheek, long nails digging into the soft, untarnished flesh of his neck.

"Ivan—" Roman began.

"No!" Nikolai protested, shoving Roman's hand away from his face. Roman took a step back.

"Tell me what you want from me, and you'll have it. Do you want me to take my place upon the throne again and help keep the balance—" he stuttered when he spoke of balance. "Do you want me to wait until the sun rises and my flesh melts from my body? Do you want me to find a nice, thick rope and hang myself from these very rafters? I will do what you ask of me."

Silence reigned for a few moments.

A cruel grin spread over Roman's lips. "Why, dear brother, you're in love with her."

Ivan laughed loudly.

"I'm..." Nikolai was once again at a loss for words.

Was he?

"But is she in love with you?" Roman leaned in close to Nikolai, their noses a centimeter apart. His eyes moved to Æsa first, then his whole body followed like a puppet on strings. Once again at her side, Roman leaned over the tub and reached his hand out. Æsa flinched, as did Nikolai.

When his large hand touched her cheek, she bared her teeth in a show of aggression and disgust. He did not move his hand away or show offense in the way she reacted. Though Roman had wanted Nikolai to kill Æsa and himself, it was obvious that this new piece of information delighted him—to discover that Nikolai loved her was something entirely new.

Nikolai hadn't really known, not until Roman said it.

"Tell me, Æsa, do you love my little brother?"

Nikolai desperately needed to know, regardless of the answer, regardless of the outcome. Her eyes darted to his for the shortest of seconds.

"No," she told Roman, her words calculated. When the smug grin appeared on Roman's face, she added, "Not in the way...you speak of love. I lost the ability to love when my family was killed, when each of my Sisters were devoured, tortured, and strung up to dry in the scorching summer sun. I lost the ability to feel such things. I forgot how to feel after ten years of silence, of loneliness. But Nikolai enabled me to feel something again. That's the difference between you and me, Roman. I lost my family and would do anything to have them back. You have a family, and you've done everything to force them away. You should be ashamed of yourself."

Nikolai didn't know what Æsa felt; she did not love him, but she only felt something because of him. If that was not love, what was it? He had not expected her to answer yes, but he had not expected her answer to be as powerful as it was. He felt something in her words: not quite hope, but something close to it. She had a spark inside her that would help her weather this storm, even if he didn't make it. Roman would admire that spark.

But he often killed what he admired.

"Star-crossed lovers." Roman chuckled. "Well, this changes everything... Ivan, you brought some books on Sirens, did you not?"

"Yes, Brother."

"Bring them to us," Roman commanded.

Ivan returned with three books, and Roman picked up the chair and beckoned Nikolai to sit. When he refused, Roman shoved him down. They both knew who would win the physical fight. Every action Nikolai considered would likely result in consequences for Æsa, the only person he wanted to make it out of this unharmed.

Roman stood beside the chair, hand clutched tight around Nikolai's shoulder.

Roman took the smallest book, flipping it open with one hand. Nikolai recognized it from his childhood home. His mother used to read it to him when he was a child. Seeing it now in the hands of the very person who had killed her dazed Nikolai. The little blue book did not belong in this room, amongst this horror.

"*Sirens are said to be the reincarnation of drowned women,*" Roman read aloud. "*A Siren's kiss can heal wounds.*' All fascinating, don't you think,

Nikolai? Do you believe these legends? Do you believe Mother came back as one? Perhaps we should see if Æsa's kiss can fix you."

Nikolai balled his hands into fists atop his thighs.

Next, Ivan presented a large book with a tattered brown leather cover and broken bindings. This book had been opened many times by many villains scouring its pages for the next cruel method to use against Sirens —the wicked men adding more to the book, page by page by endless page.

Ivan stared at Æsa. "I took this one from Eiríkur's personal collection."

The book groaned as the leather was stretched open after years of being shut. Faded and worn, stained with blood. Black blood. Ivan flipped to a page that depicted horrid drawings of a tail, the scales ripped off to reveal the soft flesh beneath. He showed it to both Nikolai and Æsa like he was reading to children.

"Scale prying. Eiríkur wished to know what lay underneath," Ivan explained, moving to another page. Each new form of horror had detailed notes about each Siren being tortured. "Did you know Eiríkur demanded that Árelía have hands like his? He split the webbing of her fingers not long after their marriage—not extensively painful at first. But when she swam, it felt like daggers between her fingers. You must know what it is like for a Siren who is unable to swim, yes?"

Æsa didn't reply, didn't even look at him. She stared intently at the book, her wet fingers reaching for the pages, her palm pressing against the drawn Siren hand without webbing.

"Now, my personal favorite..." Ivan flipped the pages along, opening it to one that had a depiction of a Siren across both pages, her tail split unevenly, resembling a disturbing, gruesome version of human legs. "Fin splitting. I think this one is quite fitting for our current situation. If I can perfect the fin splitting, you and Nikolai can be together."

39

ÆSA

At the mention of the fin splitting, Nikolai erupted from his chair, lunging for Ivan. He shoved him hard against the basin, splashing water out of the sides and thrashing Æsa inside of it. The book toppled over and sank into the water, pages upon pages of horrors destroyed.

She looked at those pages being taken back by the water and remembered her Sisters. The things they always said about the Queen stolen from the Sea.

"She will suffer up there, but she did it for us."

"She will never be happy. They will never understand our kind."

"Man corrupts everything."

Ivan and Nikolai tumbled, wrestling with one another. Æsa watched Nikolai clamber on top of his brother, pummeling him as fast and hard as he could until the crack of a tooth and the gargle of blood could be heard in the small room.

"Enough," Roman shouted. He reached for Nikolai's shirt collar, yanking him back so hard that it left a mark on his throat. Throwing Nikolai onto his back, Roman stomped on his chest, making him gasp for air. Keeping his foot there, Roman scowled at him. "Always making a scene, Nikolai. It seems it's time for you to be put in your room. We'll let Ivan have his turn with the Siren."

Nikolai shoved Roman's foot from his chest and rolled onto all fours as he tried to get back up. Roman yanked him to his feet and dragged him from the room.

"You never did learn to share," Roman commented viciously as he departed the room with Nikolai in his grasp.

The door slammed.

Nikolai's shouting didn't stop. Æsa could hear it clearly, followed by a groan, then silence. She shut her eyes and tried not to think of what might have happened, feeling the world close in on her. Living in the deep by herself for ten years had made darkness something she welcomed; to feel it around her for a few moments relaxed her. However, in the vast, dark ocean, she would open her eyes and see nothing. Now, when she opened her eyes, she saw Ivan.

Spitting out a tooth, Ivan wiped his mouth with the back of his hand. He glared at Æsa, a grin on his blood-stained lips. "We are alone at last."

"What will you do with him?" she asked.

Ivan raised an eyebrow. "I'm about to split your fin, and you ask about Nikolai?"

She waited.

"I am going to have to work extra hard to ensure you understand that you should be worrying about yourself, Siren." Ivan pointed his bloodied finger at her. "Looks like you've already faced death before. You've got a fighting spirit."

Ivan turned to the door, disappearing for a few seconds before returning with a leather case, a small table, and a gurney. His arms flexed as he lowered the table, flipping it so that it was upright, and placed the leather case upon it. From the bag, he began to withdraw metal tools that glimmered in the lantern light. A few different blades, a needle and thread, ointment, salve, and scissors.

"Now." Ivan turned around. "Either you cooperate, or I use the chloroform. And I would much rather you be awake for this."

She did not move as he approached. She scratched at him when he reached for her, lunging at him in the hope of doing enough damage to stop him. He grabbed her hand, bending it back at the wrist. She cried out in pain, and he grabbed her throat, bringing her head down hard against the edge of the tank.

Her vision blurred; she felt her consciousness falter and catch. Stunned, she was paralyzed as Ivan brought her out of the basin, water sloshing on the floor.

Æsa could still feel his hands, which meant she would be able to feel the pain. She writhed in his arms, trying to get away from his grip. Ivan slammed her to the table. The gasp from her lips was cut short, air unable to enter her chest. Ivan leaned over her, his hand on her throat, their noses almost touching, "I know exactly how to keep you alive yet immobile, on that delicate line of life and death. Don't test me, Siren."

She lolled her head to the side and groaned, a searing throb pulsing through the spot where she had been hit. The cold leather slapped around her stomach, and she frantically tried to get away. White hair flew in a frenzy as she tried to escape, regaining her senses as adrenaline pulsed through her. This was what real fear felt like. Acting tough in front of Roman had been easier when she thought there was hope.

But that hope fizzled out like fire in water.

Pinned down onto the table by three leather straps, Æsa looked away from Ivan as he grabbed his first tool. The scissors made sickly slicing noises, cutting the air between the blades.

"They start with the scissors," he explained, "so that the delicate end of the tail is cut evenly. Once we move further up, then I will use the scalpels."

Æsa silently cried, hating to let Ivan see her fear. But he was not looking at her face; he was staring at her strapped-down tail, one of the few parts of her body that was still pristine and beautiful. He palmed the end, holding it flat against the table and smoothing it out gently, then brought the scissors right to the center. Æsa stared hard at the wall as if somehow it might burst, and she could be free.

Snip.

Æsa wished to be strong, but a scream erupted from her. She shook violently as she tried to get away from the pain. Her hands clutched tightly into fists. A cry came from her throat, loud and long. Her eyes remained open the entire time; she dared not close them.

Snip.

The white-hot pain coursed through her entire tail, sending waves of agony through her body. The tail was the most sensitive part of a Siren's body, delicate at the bottom, where it was fleshy and flexible. Higher up, it had a protective layer of thick scales; they would be much harder to cut through, but with more flesh to go through, this would be the most painful. That and when Ivan began to slowly relocate her spine as he kept it to one side.

Snip.

Tears streaked her face; her ears no longer heard her own screams.

Snip.

"I have a secret to tell you," Ivan said as though he wasn't deforming her but rather having afternoon tea. "Our mother was never scared of Nikolai. She loved him more than the rest of us, even after he killed our father. You see, when you tell someone something over and over, they start to believe it. That's what we did to him. And Siren, I'll tell you this: you're not going to survive this whole procedure."

Snip.

"You're not going to survive," he taunted again. "You are not going to survive, Siren."

Snip.

"There." Ivan was finished for the day. "We can't do too much in one sitting, Siren. We need you to heal up nice now."

She held back sobs, but they still raked through her body.

"Some ointment—this may sting a little." He snickered. "I'm going to cauterize this section instead of sewing it. It's far too delicate and fragile for a needle and thread."

"He's going to kill you," she mumbled almost incoherently.

"You're familiar with the feeling of being burned, so you know what's coming," he said, ignoring her comment. When he finally did press the hot metal to her tail, he did so with more force than he needed, her tail melting to the table.

40

NIKOLAI

Being burned by the sunlight was horrible, an experience Nikolai would never wish upon anyone. Being starved had been torturous, but once your mind started to fade in and out between sanity, you stopped thinking too much about the empty vat in your stomach. Being beaten into submission was not new to Nikolai. Watching someone cut off Sif's head had been traumatizing, disturbing on the highest level.

But listening to Æsa's screaming in the room next to his was by far the worst thing Nikolai had ever experienced.

Having to hear someone you loved being hurt by your own family because of your own incompetence. That was the worst thing of all.

Her screams penetrated the walls with ease. Weakly, he slumped against the closest wall to where Æsa was. He deserved to hear everything that was happening, to wonder what part of her body was being mutilated, what Ivan was doing and saying to her. With uncovered ears, blood dripping from his mouth from where his cheek had been ripped by connecting with his teeth, his nose broken, jaw fractured, Nikolai wished he was suffering for Æsa. If he could take her pain—all of it—he would.

Tears slid from his eyes.

He couldn't sit around any longer. He crawled over to the door. It had a typical keyhole, and Nikolai searched for something to pick the lock: a nail, a splinter of wood—anything. Crawling along, he scoured for a nail not deeply embedded in the wood, but it was to no avail. No nail could be pried from these planks of wood with only his fingers.

Fingers.

Nikolai looked down at his own hand and realized the sacrifice he would have to make to save Æsa. It was no different from anything else he had already sacrificed for her. His own safety, Kashmir, Mihai, Otávia. What was one finger?

Left index finger. It had to go. Using his teeth, he clamped down at the lowest knuckle of his finger. He pushed through instinct and self-preservation a bit harder. Skin, tendon, bone, cartilage. His teeth met at last, and the severed finger remained in his mouth. He felt the blood replenish him.

Spitting his finger out of his mouth, Nikolai began to peel back the flesh away from the bone. Tiny bones, to be dealt with delicately. He had other fingers to sacrifice should this one not work, but he never wanted to do that again. When the bone was exposed, Nikolai cleaned the blood from it on his shirt and wiped his hands. Blood gushed from his stub of a finger, and he took a small drink from it, savoring it, before covering the wound with a piece of his shirt.

Snapping the tiny bone broke it into a few shards. They were almost too small, but Nikolai knew he had to make it work. He picked out the longest, sharpest fragment and one more for good measure. He began to work the lock, managing to open it despite his shaking hands. Relief flooded him, and he felt suddenly as though he had the energy to survive this, to save Æsa from his brothers. One room over, he noticed the door had not been locked on the outside—all he had to do was turn the handle.

Ivan was covered in Æsa's blood, seemingly unfazed by the scent. She was strapped down to the table, her tail currently being cauterized. Ivan stopped when he heard the door open. "Brother, she's a tough one."

"I know," Nikolai said with a growl.

Ivan's eyes bulged from his skull. Scowling, he reached for a blade. Nikolai stepped into the room and grabbed his own blade, attacking his brother. He knew his weak spots, how his confidence overtook his intelligence in a fight. Ducking a swipe from Ivan's blade, Nikolai kneed him in the stomach and then spun around, disarming him in the process.

Ivan chuckled, always trying to appear as though everything went how he wanted it to, as though he had known Nikolai would do this. But it was his way of hiding his real thoughts and fears, his worry that he might not survive this. Roman felt no fear: that was where they were different. Ivan wanted to be like Roman, but Nikolai could smell his fear.

"I should kill you right here," Nikolai growled.

"Do it. You don't have the guts, Brother." Ivan laughed.

"I need you alive for what comes next." Nikolai looked at the door. He shouted, "Roman!"

Confident, brisk footfalls could be heard from the hallway before Roman appeared. His normally calm demeanor was upturned rapidly when he saw the threat at hand, and for the first time in Nikolai's memory, Roman looked worried. He raised a hand. "Nikolai, I think hunger has gone to your head. That's your brother you hold. Let me get you something to eat."

"I want Æsa freed," he said. "I want her untouched, unharmed any further than the damage Ivan has done, and I want her to be left alone by the likes of you."

"Done." Roman wouldn't gamble with Ivan's life; that was his weakness. He held on dearly to the only family member who still had his back. "But I get *you*. Your punishment will be death by sun."

"Done."

"No," Æsa moaned, turning her head to look at Nikolai. "No, Nikolai, please... I'm... I'll be alone. I'm not worth your life."

"We make a blood oath. If either of us breaks it, we both die." Nikolai kept both arms wrapped around Ivan but brought the blade to his own hand, slicing his palm.

Roman picked up another knife, cutting his hand across a scar.

"Put it down now," Nikolai commanded.

Roman obeyed, crossing to Nikolai.

They pressed together their sliced open palms.

"Alligant dictum sanguine nostro," Roman said.

Nikolai repeated the words.

It looked as though life was taken out of them as magic rippled through the room. They were bound by blood; neither could betray the other.

"When the sun sets, we will return her to the ocean," Roman said with a sneer. "Like a happy family."

"Minus one." Nikolai slit Ivan's throat.

Roman erupted in anger, but he could do nothing. Not yet. He dropped to his knees beside his dying brother. Ivan's hands clutched Roman's jacket, pulling him close in fear and desperation. Nikolai watched as Roman pressed his head to Ivan's. He spoke softly to his dying brother, soothing words surely meaning nothing to him.

When life faded from Ivan's eyes, Roman looked up at Nikolai, the essence of desperation on his features. He asked coldly, "Why?"

"He hurt Æsa."

41

ÆSA

Æsa wept quietly on the table. Strapped down, the foul scent of blood—hers and Ivan's—was all she could smell. But she didn't cry for herself; she cried for Nikolai. He had once asked her how much more he needed to do to prove she was worth saving, but she had never expected this.

Roman rose to his feet. Æsa turned her head and looked at the two remaining brothers. Knowing that Nikolai could not slip away with the blood bond sealed, he carried Ivan's body from the room and left them alone.

Nikolai still held the knife in his hand. He wavered where he stood before stepping toward Æsa to untie her. He collapsed to the ground, the knife clattering along the floor. Groaning from his place on the ground, Nikolai tried to bring himself to his feet again and failed. The last of his energy had been used to kill Ivan. He palmed the little blue book Roman had read from and pulled it toward him.

"Æsa," he mumbled. "He believes it all..."

It didn't make sense to Æsa, but she clung to those words, held them tight in her mind where they would not be forgotten. Nothing Nikolai had ever said to her or done for her would be forgotten. After several long, grueling minutes, Nikolai got back onto his knees, planting his hand on the table and hoisting himself back up.

Æsa's eyes met his, sadness filling them both. With a gentleness to his movements, Nikolai began to undo the bonds that held her down. He tightened his hand on the leather belt, teeth grinding together as he looked upon her fresh wounds.

"I'm sorry this happened to you." His voice shook. "I'm going to make it right."

Æsa sat up, wavering slightly as sharp pain emitted from her tail and ran the length of her spine. Resting her hand upon Nikolai's shoulder, she leaned against his chest. She breathed in his scent so that she could remember it forever—metallic blood with an earthy musk that had always surrounded him. He stroked his hand along her back, comforting her; it almost felt as though they would find a way out of this. She knew they wouldn't. A blood bond could not be broken.

"Your mother wasn't afraid of you," she whispered gently.

"What are you talking about?" Nikolai tilted her chin up so he could look into her eyes.

She leaned her cheek into the palm of his hand. Warm and calloused, it felt like home. "Ivan told me. They lied to you."

He inhaled deeply. "None of that matters anymore."

They held one another in silence for a long time. He ran his hand along the puckered skin on her back, long rippling scars like sand when the waves pulled it along the shore. She rested her head against his chest, listening to his heart beating; his heart was good. In another world, another time, they might have been given the chance to be happy. But the world was cruel, ripping goodness and happiness from the clutches of anyone who dared pursue it. It was impossible to achieve, yet Man, Vampire, and Siren alike sought it.

Hope—that was what fueled them all.

The door opened, and a ragged-looking Roman entered. Hair disheveled, his knuckles bloodied, Æsa realized the rage was inherited in the brothers, even if it appeared in different ways.

"It's time," Roman growled.

"I want to see the sunrise," Nikolai admitted. "I've heard it is beautiful."

Roman ran his bloodied hands through his hair. "I will grant you that."

Before he left the room, he threw a metal container at Nikolai. Nikolai caught the flask, shaking it to hear the liquid sloshing within. Quickly, with the demeanor of an excited child, he unscrewed the cap and threw back the contents. The small amount of blood was enough to replenish him for a moment. Once the last drop was upon his tongue, he threw the flask down.

Lifting Æsa, Nikolai carried her out the door. The stifling scent of death faded the moment they were in the hall, the fresher air allowing a fraction of the tension to release from their bodies.

Neither of them knew where they were but suspected no one was left within. At least no one alive. Roman had likely kept the human alive for blood or perhaps to use him for traveling during daylight.

He stood by the door, his hands gloved but clearly swollen. "This way, Brother."

"I'm not your brother," Nikolai spat.

"You can deny it all you want, but we are blood. And blood is thicker than *water*." He hissed the last word, his eyes on Æsa.

Nikolai said nothing else as they followed Roman from the house. Darkness swept over the land, blanketing everything. A carriage sat, far nicer than Nikolai's had been, with two beautiful horses standing patiently in front of it.

A tank was in the back, a generosity extended by Roman that was quite unexpected. Nikolai slipped Æsa inside, but she clutched hard at him, not wanting to let him go. He pried her hands away but climbed in the back beside her.

The sound of the water lapping at the shore did not bring Æsa joy this time, only anguish. Roman looked grim when he opened the door. Although he would finally get the chance to kill Nikolai, it had cost him Ivan. There were no winners in this war.

Beckoning for them to leave the carriage, they obeyed. Once again, Nikolai carried Æsa down to the ocean, this time for good. Roman gave them space. He would get what he wanted in a few hours when the sun rose.

"You're strong," Nikolai told her as he waded through the shallow water. Giant rocks hung around the cove, gray in the absence of light. The water was dark blue, almost black, though it would glitter brilliantly in the sun. The sun that would soon be his demise. "Stronger than anyone I've ever met."

"Do you think this will bring balance?" she asked.

"I don't know if there ever has been a balance," he admitted. "I think it's simply a way to keep us hoping that things will get better."

"Things were better while I was with you." She kissed him, her lips parting against his, stubble tickling her scarred flesh. She wished she had power, power to absorb his pain.

But she had no power.

42

NIKOLAI

There was nothing either of them could say. Words held no power anymore.

Roman sat at the edge of the carriage, watching them. As the morning arrived, he disappeared inside, safe and secure.

For one placid fraction of a second, Nikolai saw the sun. Bright orange and perfectly round, rising above the horizon. The skies all around the sun were orange and pink, yellow and purple. A combination of colors more beautiful than any moonlight or Nightsun he had seen his entire life. And in front of all that beauty was Æsa, her bright white hair illuminated, shining so bright he couldn't see her features.

But he already knew she was more beautiful than the sun.

His body was exposed, upper half nude, tattered trousers covering his legs. After the split second of awe at the beauty of the sunrise, pain came. White hot agony coursed through his veins as his flesh felt like it was being peeled off. He leaned forward, unleashing a gut-wrenching cry of pain.

Charred flesh peeled from his body, his once handsome face blackened by the sun. He slumped forward into the water, still clinging to life for a moment. His head fell as the sun finished him. Pain lingered, somehow less now; his body twitched, and the screaming stopped. He kept his eyes open; they met with Æsa's, and then...

The night was gone.

- Æsa

Silence.

Æsa stared at what was left of Nikolai. Something vital was missing inside her, like a part of her burned with him. It was something time would never heal, just as time never healed the part of her that died with her Sisters. She crawled out of the water, lay beside what was left of his body, and held him as waves lapped at her tail.

She felt something dig against her as the sun continued to rise. Lifting her upper half up, choking back a sob, she withdrew the tattered and ash-covered blue book. Blinking back what was left of her tears, she palmed the book. Something clicked as she flipped it open. Though she could not read the words, the images were clear.

Some believed a Siren's kiss could heal wounds.

"He believes it all." Nikolai's words played in her mind.

Æsa waited for the sun to set.

When it did, Roman emerged to see his brother lying dead on the ground, nearly unidentifiable except for his sky-blue eyes. He walked over to the cadaver, ignoring Æsa as she scrambled back into the water to get away from him. Roman shoved Nikolai onto his back, leaning over to ensure that his brother was truly dead. Then his eyes moved along the shore, over the foamy waves that licked Nikolai's extended hand, and landed on Æsa.

"You stay out of trouble now," he told her, a comical tone to his voice, yet he sounded broken, too. What did he have left? A fallen Brotherhood somewhere in Osleka.

"Come." Æsa beckoned for Roman, swimming close to the shore so that when she sat, her upper body was exposed to the cool night air.

He approached; whether it was to show he was not afraid of her or because he was truly intrigued, she did not know. Face to face, Roman crouched in the shallows, his eyes vicious. When Æsa reached for him, he recoiled. She gently grabbed his hands; the smooth lamb-skin gloves were the softest things she'd felt in a long time. Slowly, she peeled away the gloves, finger by finger, revealing the gruesome nails beneath.

The black gloves floated away on the foamy waves.

"A Siren's kiss is said to heal," she whispered, her gentle fingers moving over the open wounds on his knuckles.

She flicked her eyes up to meet his, stricken by how much they looked like Nikolai's. "May I?"

"And why would you tend to my wounds?" he asked, skeptical.

"You withheld your end of the deal. You got me here," she explained, hoping it would be enough.

"But I killed Nikolai."

"He would have done it himself after he saved me. We both know that." She wondered if this was true. "It was inevitable."

"You are wise, Æsa." He was intrigued, hungry for her kiss. "But I know your kiss can't heal my hands."

"It will heal your heart." She looked deep into his eyes, hoping he would believe her.

Something flashed in his features; he wanted to believe. "That part of me is well beyond healing, my dear."

"Let me try." She snaked her hand behind his neck, feeling the soft hairs growing in. Her other hand reached up to cup his face, angling him so she could kiss him. When his blue eyes closed, Æsa bit down as hard as she could upon her own tongue. She no longer needed it—she would not speak without Nikolai. The pain was nothing compared to having her tail sliced open, and she managed to sever her tongue from her body without screaming in pain. She kissed Roman hard, forcing the blood deep into his mouth.

He shoved her away, and she stared up at him as he began to choke. Black blood smeared over her face; she spat out her own tongue and watched as it floated on the water before sinking slowly. Roman stumbled, trying to vomit up the blood, but it was already killing him. His wild, crazed eyes looked at Æsa with hatred. Dropping to his knees, he wheezed and then fell face down, black froth at his lips.

A wind blew, chilling Æsa, reminding her she was still alive. Blood pulsed through the stem of her tongue, still gushing. Spitting it out over and over, she wondered if she could die of the blood loss. She didn't care what happened now. She believed it was her own blood that created a balance that day, though the balance had never been about her or about Sirens.

She floated on her back, staring up at the star-scattered sky above her.

"Sister."

"It's her."

"Æsa." Their words were calming, soothing. *"It's her."*

"Æsa," they called again. *"She's home."*

"Æsa, you're home."

Hands wrapped themselves around Æsa's body, gently touching her, pulling her down beneath the blood-filled water surface. She sank deep into the water, hands enveloping her in touch. Blackness consumed her, but she could still feel and hear them.

Her Sisters.

EPILOGUE

When Eiríkur's blood was spilled, the balance was shifted back into place.

Those who lived only for Siren flesh forgot the taste. Those who wanted them for show discovered there were other, better ways to draw a crowd. Those who kept them as décor in their home came to prefer plants. Hunters went back to being fishermen, renaming their ships after their daughters, mothers, and wives.

Man went back to the mundane.

It had been a year since Nikolai died for her. What Æsa learned in a year of living among the Sirens who survived the genocide was that she could have many families in her life—her Sisters, Nikolai, and now she was once again home in the arms of her Sisters. She had been given so many chances.

"Æsa." Eyvör—one of the only survivors Æsa knew from her past, had surprised her a year ago, alive and well—touched her tattooed arm gently. Three solid rings on her bicep for Nikolai, Pure Blooded. A single ring on the other bicep for Kashmir, pure of heart. "The Song is starting. We'd like you to confirm that we have everything right."

She nodded. They dove deep from the cove and into the waters, along the shore of rocks like giant titans protecting them. The first one to arrive many years ago was Eyvör. She had a similar story to Æsa's—about a Nightwalker who was kind, who protected her at all costs with no need of thanks. Eyvör was a beacon to the others, a new leader for those who flocked to the cove for safety.

Two others were brought forth by Nikolai—Lýra and Læla.

There were thirty Sirens there, and all of them turned to Æsa when she showed up. Some looked nervous, some brave, and others looked at her battle scars with pride, proud to say she was part of their family. Since she could not sing, they sang to her. When they did, she could remember Nikolai through their words.

To them, he, too, was family.

THE SONG OF THE SEA

Man came with greed
Man came with hunger

They took our Sisters
They took our Song

When the Song of the Sea
was no longer
We hid deep without pride
without honor

He came from darkness
He came from night
Extended his hand
to make things right

He asked for naught
but gave us all
He saved our Sisters
'til the day of his fall

The Song of the Sea

*Through the night
we remember him
and the greed he did fight
with the good within*

*He gave his life
for our Sister*

*His blood was spilled
for the balance*

ACKNOWLEDGMENTS

To Cassandra, Tiff, Stephen, Alma, Stefanie, Fay. Without this incredible team, The Blood Bound Series wouldn't have been able to exist the way it does.

To all those who have been there from the beginning and those who came along the way, thank you for all your support.

Writing a book is a very individualized process, but publishing one requires every single one of you.

INDEX A

THE BLOOD BOUND SERIES TIMELINE

<u>The Year of the Curse</u> (1504) Azalea Luca's time/Blood Coven

<u>The Year of the Pines</u> (1781) Torenia is 7/Ashen Heart

<u>The Year of Ash</u> (1783) Song of the Sea

<u>The Year of the Siren</u> (1785) Song of the Sea

<u>The Year of Gluttony</u> (1786) Song of the Sea

<u>The Year of the Raven</u> (1791) Torenia is 17/Ashen Heart

<u>The Year of the Brothers</u> (1795) Brotherhood is won

<u>The Year of Indulgence</u> (1798) Torenia meets Roman/Ashen Heart

<u>The Year of the Black Tide</u> (1808) Song of the Sea

<u>The Dark Years</u> (10 years time)

<u>The Year of the Moon</u> (1891) Red's time/Blood Coven/Blood Queen

INDEX B
TRIGGER INDEX

This book contains the following:

Blood/Gore
Flesh Eating
Suicide (Assisted)
Torture (Mental/Physical)
Violence (Fantasy)

ABOUT THE AUTHOR

Sabrina Voerman is a West Coaster with a penchant for visiting the numerous cemeteries across Vancouver Island. With a profound love of fairy tales and all things witchy, she draws her inspiration from the nature around her, allowing it to bleed into her storytelling. She is always seeking new adventures and places to explore, either in life or in her writing. When she isn't traversing all Vancouver Island has to offer, she can be found with a cup of coffee either reading a book or writing one.

THANK YOU FOR READING

Thank you for reading *Song of the Sea*. We deeply appreciate our readers, and are grateful for everyone who takes the time to leave us a review. If you're interested, please visit our website to find review links. Your reviews help small presses and indie authors thrive, and we appreciate your support.

Other Titles by Quill & Crow

Ashen Heart

The Bone Key

The Ancient Ones Trilogy